RAVENSWOOD MURDERS

An absolutely gripping crime thriller with a massive twist

HELEN H. DURRANT

Detective Alice Rossi Book 2

JOFFE BOOKS

Joffe Books, London
www.joffebooks.com

First published in Great Britain in 2023

© Helen H. Durrant 2023

Cover Design by Nick Castle

ISBN: 978-1-83526-209-2

PROLOGUE

I know you'll come and when you do I want things to be simple. It won't be easy. I won't be here to tell you what happened. I'll be dead, lifeless in a cold grave. That is why I plan to leave what few clues I can for you to find and act upon.

He's told me the ill treatment he metes out is no more than I deserve, that I and the others here can't be trusted and will get what's coming to us. I've asked him what we've done, screamed at him to tell me why I'm here but he just laughs and tells me to work it out.

Work what out? I'm at a loss to know what he means. During those first few days of captivity I was angry, confused and convinced he'd got it wrong. I thought he'd mistaken me for someone else. But he insists that's not the case.

I know there are others here but he does not allow us even to catch sight of one another, let alone talk. But a while back he called one of the other girls by her name — *Josie* — and that rang a bell. Rang it so loud I heard the echo for days.

Because then I understood.

I knew a Josie once, in another life. I want to ask him if it's her but I'm scared of his reply. Because if it is her then he'll never let me or the others go. But the big question is — why now? Why wait all this time before doing something about us?

I have tried to escape but all my attempts have failed. All I got was bruises from the beatings he gave me, and the lack of food and water made me sick. Now I try other things, things to annoy him. I call to the others hoping that some brave soul might reply. I spit out the sleeping pills he feeds me every night. That does make him angry. Last week he lashed out, knocked me to the floor badly injuring my leg. Now I can hardly walk, never mind escape.

If I'm right, there will be five of us being held here. I believe he is disposing of us one by one. What happened was a while ago, and since then my life has been hard. I've lived on the streets, been heavily into drugs and try as I might, apart from Josie, I can't recall their names. Once we were friends, close even. My one wish before I die is that I can speak to Josie about my suspicions. But even that possibility has been snatched away from me.

Josie was a model prisoner, not like me. She was quiet and I never heard her answer back. In fact, I never heard a peep out of her until the day she died. That day her screams brought the place down. When I asked, he said she didn't suffer. He said the knife was at her throat before she knew what was happening. I don't believe that either. I heard the noise she made and I saw the aftermath. He made me clean up the blood. I scrubbed and scrubbed but some of it still stains the stone flags outside my locked door.

Soon it will be my turn and I wonder how and when it will happen. I doubt he'll make it quick like Josie's was. He hates me and anyway he's not a kind man, he enjoys being cruel and he's good at it.

The one thing that bothers me is that I can't remember his name. I knew it once but my brain is addled from all the drugs I've taken. I know he was a dealer on the estate, he supplied all the kids, including me. But I have to try and get that name back. I have to help the people investigating our disappearance so they can catch him. They must know the truth about what he did. If by some fluke I am found, or they understand the message I leave behind, then the girls still imprisoned here will have a chance of freedom.

It won't be long now. I'm a difficult prisoner. After he pushed me to the floor, I picked myself up and kicked him on the shin, making him cry out. That's why I'm being punished, why I sit alone in the dark, stitching my own shroud.

CHAPTER ONE

One week later

Monday

DCI Alice Rossi tore her eyes from the freshly dug hole and raised them to the trees where the pale sunlight barely filtered through. She felt uneasy. Was it the place itself, or the knowledge of what must have gone on here? Probably a bit of both.

"This is the perfect place to hide the dead, isn't it, off the beaten track. No one ever comes here," Superintendent Leo Monk noted.

"Why d'you reckon they choose one particular tree and not the others?" she said.

Superintendent Monk threw her a puzzled look. What the hell was she talking about?

"The birds. Look. There are at least half a dozen ravens in that tree over there, but none anywhere else."

He shrugged. "Maybe it's their preferred roosting spot."

Alice wondered if that's what these woods were to the killer, his preferred burial spot. Something to consider. All the bodies found so far had been buried here.

It was a late summer's evening in pretty woodland surroundings. Tranquil, innocent even. But they were far from that. Alice felt a sudden chill run through her body. She pulled her jacket around her. "This place is evil. Don't you feel it?"

"It's not the place that's evil, Alice. It's what's been done here."

But Alice didn't believe it was that alone. Places — woodland, a hillside or a house — had an evil all their own. She'd felt it on Needle Crag, above the Still Waters rural retreat, during her last case.

"We were lucky. A local man walking his dog earlier found the grave," she told Superintendent Leo Monk. "She wasn't buried deep and the animal kept sniffing the spot, refusing to budge when it was called."

"Clever dog."

"Dr Dolly Parkes thinks she died no more than a week ago. Her carotid artery was severed almost in two. She'll know more after the autopsy. Finding her so soon after death gives us a chance of identifying this one."

"Same killer?"

"I reckon so. It shows the same hallmarks as the other three that were found in these woods. The body had lime spread over it and he'd broken her teeth and sewn up her mouth," she said softly. "Her hands were missing too, just like the others. Horrendous to look at. I'm just hoping Dolly will confirm that it was done post-mortem like the others."

Monk looked down at the hole in the ground. "Poor girl."

Alice bent to go under the police tape. "Dolly will do her best for us. I know her of old and she always goes the extra mile. And Dr Jack Nevin and his forensics team will go over every millimetre of this area with a fine toothcomb. If the killer has left any trace, they'll find it."

"Yes, they're a good team," he said. "Both Parkes and Nevin are outstanding in their fields."

"And they're both old friends of mine." She smiled. "During my time in the force we've worked on a number of cases together, and I've always thought highly of their work."

"You also have a sound track record, Alice. Which is why you're now the senior investigating officer on the Dream Catcher operation."

Alice wasn't sure how to take that. Monk had intended it as a reward but Alice felt like she'd been handed a poisoned chalice. Solving this case would involve days of work with precious little to go on. There were times when she wished he'd chosen someone else for the task.

"Until now, you have just been reading the case files, the witness statements and the like. This new find will throw you right into the thick of things. You okay with that?" Monk asked her.

Alice nodded. "As you say, I've done my homework and I've seen the killer's handiwork for myself. Now I know what we're up against. Believe me, Leo, I'm determined to get the fiend who snatched these girls' lives from them in this horrible way."

Alice had spent the last month with her head in the paperwork generated by this case. It was heart-wrenching reading, this tale of kidnap and murder involving teenage girls. There were no witnesses and nothing left on the bodies to identify them. What she wanted more than anything was to give them all names, tell their relatives that they'd been found. They needed a proper burial, not a hastily dug hole in public woodland.

Not only did the girls not have names but they'd no idea how many the killer had taken. They had a long list of girls reported missing in the Greater Manchester area who fitted the profile, but to date, apart from the discovery of this body and three others, they were no further on. Once the girls disappeared, that was it — nothing. No demands for ransom, no phone calls. It was as if they simply vanished into thin air. And since none of them had been identified, they couldn't investigate possible links between them either.

"The press gets wind of this latest find and they'll be on your tail," Monks said.

Alice nodded. "I want this discovery staying under wraps for as long as possible. I don't want them to know we're interested in this location either. The less the killer thinks we know about what he's doing the better."

Monk looked doubtful. "It'll give you an edge of sorts but you won't be able to keep it secret for long. Information about the other three bodies was leaked to the press, and not by us."

"You're thinking the killer himself?"

"The team are sound so I can't think who else it could be." Monk cleared his throat. "I'm afraid he knows about you too."

A shiver went down Alice's spine. It took a lot to frighten her but this wasn't good. The last killer she'd brought to book had known all about her too and it had given the evil woman a huge advantage. "How?"

"We have no idea. Be aware that he may try to contact you too. I had the handwriting in the letter he sent me analysed, and our expert believes it was written by a man. Not only did he boast about what he'd done but he gave specific details too, so it was definitely the killer that sent it."

Alice had seen the letter in the case file. It consisted of a lengthy diatribe written in black fountain-pen ink, the letters scratchy and old-fashioned looking. "No doubt he thinks murdering young girls is impressive. Well, we'll catch the bastard, and then he'll see how impressed we are."

"Better not get too emotionally involved, Alice," Leo Monk advised. "I know how hard that is in a case like this. Try to concentrate on the facts, and keep your emotions out of it."

Easier said than done. The girl that had been lying in this hole was no age. She'd had her entire life in front of her. The killer had stolen that from her and deserved all that was coming his way.

"You'll know from the file that the other three girls had been in the ground longer than this one. The first two were found two months back and the third a couple of months before then. All of them were buried in these woods."

"No chance of identifying any of them, I suppose?"

"The bodies were too far gone. Like this one, the bodies had been covered in lime, which speeds up decomposition and helps prevent odours. Jack Nevin did a DNA check but there were no matches on the database. You've read the reports — no possessions were found either. It was impossible to get any dental records as the teeth had been smashed. Their hands had been cut off and they weren't even dressed in their own clothes, just plain white home-made gowns."

"Those weren't clothes, Leo, they look more like shrouds to me. I have an idea their captor forced the girls to sew them during their imprisonment. The gown one of the bodies was wearing had small drops of blood on it which could have come from a needle."

With a sigh Alice pushed her hands deeper into her jacket pockets. Those poor girls. What they must have suffered. "What's more, I bet they knew exactly what would happen to them once their needlework was done. What would knowing that do to a young mind?" Alice shuddered. How those girls must have agonised over their impending fate, the emotions that would have tormented them. "It takes time to sew a gown like that. He keeps them somewhere, Leo. Imprisons them and watches them suffer."

"Are you sure you're all right with this, Alice? It isn't going to be pleasant."

Alice shot him a look. "Just because I feel for their suffering, it doesn't mean I'm soft. I've dealt with all kinds of hard nuts in my time. As far as I'm concerned, the sooner we catch this one, the better. And I'm determined that my team will do just that." She looked down at the makeshift grave again. "What we have here is an opportunity to avenge these poor girls and their families."

Alice took one last look at the surroundings and started back towards the car. Despite the evening sunshine and the scenic beauty, the woodland was oppressive. What made it so was that the killer knew this area, had picked it out as a good place to bury his prey. The thought of him creeping around these trees looking for possible gravesites made her feel cold.

"I suggest you get a team in to take a closer look at these woods. It isn't too big an area," Monk said.

"I suppose so, though the team that was on the case before me did that already and they got nothing. Still, in light of the latest find we'll give it another go. As for where he was keeping the girls prior to killing them, the problem we've got is that we don't know where the killer came from. It might not be anywhere near these woods. Rochdale is that way—" she pointed — "maybe he came from there. Or it could be the Saddleworth villages, back in the other direction. Then there's the M62, which opens up a host of other possibilities. He could be from right out of the area, it's a popular spot with walkers so he might have heard of it."

"True," Monk said, "but these woods and that reservoir over there isn't somewhere you stumble on. You have to know which turning to take off the main road."

He was right. Alice had often driven right past this place without knowing it existed. It was something to bear in mind. "In any case, to reach these woods you have to take that road up there, the one from Denshaw to Newhey. Regardless of where the killer came from, he or she must have used it."

"There's no CCTV, and most of the way there aren't even any streetlights. It comes over the tops — open country. No leads there, I'm afraid, Alice. And that's the problem with this case, practically no leads at all."

A depressing thought. All they had was a killer, a man on a mission. A serial offender who went after young girls. They'd found three bodies and this one made the fourth. How many others were there, either being held or already dead?

Monk followed her to the car. "Those handmade garments, the shrouds, or whatever you call them, Forensics said they were made from old bedsheets."

"Not a good way to spend your last few days," she said. "I've just thought of something else. If the girls are being held together, then they would know when one of them was about to, well, leave the group. Horrendous. Truly awful. The sooner we stop this, Leo, the better."

"And you have my complete backing and that of the team," he said.

"Speaking of which, I intend to change things round a little," Alice said. "It's not a criticism of those who're already working the case but they've been at it a while. Fresh eyes are always a bonus in my book. I have a couple more officers I'd like to bring in."

"Certainly, appoint whoever you want to the team."

"Well, one I have in mind is a young man who's recently been promoted from Uniform to CID — DC Roger Wallis. The other is a sergeant based at the Tameside station who I worked with on the Still Waters case, one DS Jason Hawkes. He showed great promise."

CHAPTER TWO

The visit to Ravenswood over, Superintendent Monk dropped Alice back at the station in Manchester. The gruesome find and the chilling atmosphere had unnerved her, leaving Alice fit for little other than to make for home. She decided to leave the team briefing until the morning, when both she and the other members of the team would be fresh. In any case, until the post-mortem was done there was little she could add that wasn't already known to them.

Alice hadn't yet spoken to DS Jason Hawkes about his new post and wondered if this was an error on her part, particularly as his first task would be to accompany her to the girl's post-mortem. But he was young, ambitious, and would no doubt jump at the chance of working on a high-profile murder case. He'd be an asset too. He would cast much needed fresh eyes on the case and might spot things the previous team had missed.

Alice had come to know him quite well during their last case and she knew he cared about the job. Like her, he believed policing was about more than simply getting the right result. As for the rest of the team, Alice had found them jaded, dispirited by the lack of results. That had to change, and hopefully, once they had the information from

Forensics, a short pep talk would ensure that they understood the challenge ahead and what she expected of them.

At least the drive home didn't take long. Alice lived in a rambling Edwardian terrace in Openshaw on the outskirts of the city. It was handy for the station and meant she wasted little time travelling. As she pulled into the narrow driveway, she saw Dilys, her housekeeper and long-time friend, locking her front door.

"And what time d'you call this? You work too hard, Alice. I've told you before but you don't listen. You'll wear yourself out." Dilys looked her up and down. "You're in your fifties now, you know. You should be taking things a bit easier."

Fifties wasn't old these days, but Alice didn't bother to argue. It'd cut no ice with Dilys anyway. "I've got a new case to get my teeth into. That'll keep me busy and the work will keep me young."

Dilys didn't look impressed. "I've done a shop and cleaned the dining room. You should consider having that back bedroom decorated, the paper's coming away from the ceiling. Damp, I reckon."

"And you think I work hard! It sounds as if you've had a day of it. Anything in the fridge I can throw together for my supper by any chance?"

"I've done you one of them mixed salad things you like, with olives and that funny cheese. Although to my mind you could do with something a bit more substantial. And don't down too much wine. I find you asleep in the armchair again tomorrow morning, I'll have something to say."

Alice gave her a big hug. "How would I survive without you? In this insane world it's you who keeps me on the right track, but then you know that."

Looking embarrassed, Dilys shook herself free and mumbled, "Promised your mum, didn't I." With that she was gone, out into the street and straight onto the number twenty-two bus heading for Gorton.

Was Dilys right? Did she work too hard, drink too much and find her job hard to cope with? Probably, but whenever she found herself slipping, Alice recognised the signs and was the first to do something about it. The thing was, Alice loved her job and couldn't imagine doing anything else. However, there was one change she had considered making, and it was a biggy.

During these last weeks, Alice had seriously thought about selling the house and moving to a quieter part of Greater Manchester. Somewhere where there was less traffic noise and not so many pubs turning out late at night. But if she did that, what about Dilys? As it was, she was only a short bus ride away, and Alice was well aware that 'doing' for her kept her friend sane. It wasn't an easy decision to make.

Not only that, leaving this house would be a terrible wrench. She had grown up in this house, all her memories were here. It had belonged to her parents, and Alice had had a happy childhood here. All that had changed when she married Paul Hunter. By then, her parents were dead. Paul had been a controlling bully who'd done his best to rule her life, and despite her strong character, he'd almost succeeded.

Paul's untimely death had come as a huge shock. He had been an avid caver and potholer, taking risks Alice could never quite comprehend. Despite his body never being found, the coroner ruled that death had occurred as a result of a potholing accident, the infamous cave below Needle Crag being the culprit. The dreadful weather that day had made conditions even more dangerous than ever, but Paul wouldn't listen to reason. He was determined that the pothole he'd gone to explore would not win the day.

But it did, and several weeks later after some of Paul's belongings were found with his blood on them, the coroner had no choice but to rule that his death had been accidental. Naturally, the whole thing had been hugely upsetting for Alice, but at the same time she couldn't help feeling relieved. Finally, she was free and intended to remain so.

And so it was for several years until, during the Still Waters case, she made the chilling discovery that her husband was still very much alive. It changed everything. Despite his protestations to the contrary, the truth was that Paul could return at any moment. It cast a shadow over her life. Her childhood home no longer felt secure. Alice wanted to ensure that if he ever did leave his self-imposed exile and came looking for her, he wouldn't find her here.

But thoughts of the house and the nightmare of Paul's possible return were for another day. Right now Alice needed a clear head. She went indoors, kicked off her shoes and had just poured herself a generous glass of red when the front doorbell rang. What now?

"Ma'am, I hope you don't mind me calling round. I heard a rumour about your new case and fancied a word."

It was DS Jason Hawkes, the young detective who'd worked her last case with her. "Well, you heard right. I'm the new senior investigating officer on the Dream Catcher operation, and you, Sergeant, will have the dubious pleasure of being my right-hand man." She held the glass in the air. "As you see, I'm making the most of my last hours of freedom. Come tomorrow, we start in earnest and I fear we've a busy time ahead of us. Come in, have a glass yourself and I'll give you the file to take home and read."

"Thanks for putting my name forward, ma'am. I wasn't going to presume but I'm really pleased to be on the case."

Alice smiled. "You're welcome. You're a good detective. Your input on the Still Waters case was invaluable. As I recall, you saved my bacon more than once." She saw him rub the side of his head. "Still bothering you?"

"No, but I still get embarrassed when I think of how that case ended. That bang on the head was down to my own stupidity. Why did I have to trip over my big feet and knock myself out on a rock? I ask you."

Alice made a face. In fact, that wasn't quite what happened, but she wasn't going to enlighten him now. "You were lucky, it could have been worse. That crag is a weird place."

"Well, I for one won't be rushing back."

"Me neither," she said. A conversation about the crag and how the case was wound up was the last thing Alice needed right now. "You start tomorrow, eight sharp at the station for a team briefing, and then you and I go to the morgue to attend a PM. It won't be pleasant. You should read the file, understand what we're up against."

"I'll make sure I'm up to speed, ma'am."

"Good. I've asked Roger Wallis to join the team too. You'll remember him, I'm sure. He's another young detective I consider shows promise." She smiled at him. "How's your family doing?"

"Beth's going back to work part-time next week."

"And the infant, what happens to her?" she asked.

"Lizzie is going to her gran."

Alice nodded. "You're lucky. As I remember only too well from my own experience with Michael, the costs of childcare can be crippling."

"That's what Beth keeps telling me."

"D'you want that drink while you're here?" she asked.

Hawkes gave her an apologetic look. "Better not, ma'am, I'm driving. Anyway, I'd better get off. I need to pick up Lizzie and get her sorted. See you in the morning."

Alice walked down the drive with him and waved him off. He was young and resilient and he'd stood up well to the horrors of the Still Waters case, but Operation Dream Catcher was very different, inasmuch as it involved the murder of young girls. Alice downed the remainder of her wine in one. Her new team had a difficult few weeks ahead. The case would test them all, not least Alice herself.

CHAPTER THREE

The North of England Serious Murder Squad, which had recently relocated from Liverpool, was based on the fifth floor of the main police station in central Manchester. It was a convenient location for Alice in her new position as SIO in Operation Dream Catcher, as she was familiar with the building and the other teams who worked here. Unfortunately, the person she'd most been looking forward to seeing, her old boss, Superintendent Frank Osbourne, had retired. After the successful conclusion of the Still Waters case he'd decided to call it a day and end his career on a high.

Amid the noise of a dozen or so police officers all talking at the top of their voices, Alice threaded her way through the desks and computer equipment that crammed the open plan office. On the main incident board she had pinned photos and notes about the case. There wasn't much so far, just general background material that was sadly lacking in detail.

Her own office was a square at the far end that had been hived off with glass panels. Dumping her jacket and bag, she picked up the case file. Time to face the team, get this show on the road. First off she'd have to tell them about yesterday's find. Alice felt a rare flutter of nerves. She might be the SIO but at this point she was very much the new girl, this team and her were strangers. She'd no idea about their weaknesses or their strengths, nor they hers.

"Morning everyone," she began, tapping a pen on the nearest empty desktop to get their attention.

Several pairs of curious eyes swung her way. What was going on inside their heads? They all knew Monk and his reputation as a results copper. Alice was an unknown and no doubt viewed as a poor substitute. But the fact was, despite his experience and previous successes, Monk had failed to get results in the Dream Catcher case. What was the betting on her chances, she wondered, watching those curious eyes fasten on her.

"For those of you who don't know me, I'm DCI Alice Rossi, your new SIO. I'm well aware of the graft you've all put in on this case. You've worked long and hard but this morning marks a new start. I want to inject fresh impetus, a fresh approach which will hopefully yield results. With that in mind, apart from myself, we also have two new detectives joining us this morning." She introduced DS Jason Hawkes and DC Roger Wallis, who were both seated at the back of the room. "Both come with excellent records and will be an asset to the team. Make them welcome."

But instead of clapping, Alice heard the mutterings, saw the sideways looks. She groaned inwardly. This was no time for petty jealousies, she needed the entire team to work together like a well-oiled machine. Time to move on to the main business.

"Yesterday the body of a young woman was found in a shallow grave in Ravenswood, out Newhey way. The body bears all the hallmarks of our killer. It's not a break we would choose, but it's a break nonetheless, and we must make full use of it. Because she's been found so quickly, I'm hopeful that with the help of forensics we stand a good chance of identifying this one. Once we have a name, we dig into her life, speak to family, friends, anyone who knew her, in order to find out what she was doing and who she met prior to being taken. We're also after any possible links between our latest victim and the other three who've been found."

She waited to see if there were any questions but no one spoke. "DS Hawkes and I will attend the post-mortem this morning and I will brief you all after lunch. Until we have something concrete, I want everyone looking at missing persons. Concentrate on the last six months. She's no more than sixteen or seventeen so someone must be missing her. We have no idea if she's local, so cast the net wide."

"Do we know how long she's been dead, ma'am?" Roger Wallis asked.

"Not precisely, but Dr Parkes estimates not much longer than a week. Despite the damage inflicted on her face, she wasn't in the ground long enough for decomposition to have begun. That means we'll have photos."

She looked around the room. Despite the lack of questions, they appeared to be hanging onto her every word and many were taking notes. "We believe that she was held for some time prior to being killed. Hence the six-month window for the misper reports."

"What about her mouth?" Wallis asked.

She nodded. He'd done his homework. "The killer had smashed her teeth and stitched her lips together just like the others. But I'm hoping Dr Parkes can work her magic and make her look more or less presentable. I intend to put this girl's image in the papers and on the TV news. The press will ask questions, try to draw comparisons, but we tell them that she's a murder victim, nothing else."

"They're bound to ask where she was found," a young DC said.

"What's your name?"

"Detective Constable Neil Barrow, ma'am."

"Well, DC Barrow, you can tell them she was found near Rochdale but don't give them the exact location, or that this killing is like the others. And say nothing about her mouth."

"That won't put them off, ma'am. We'll have the press camping out on our doorstep, clamouring for more," he said. "This case has really caught the popular imagination."

This was always the case with murders like these. Alice couldn't understand why. The public's relish of the ghoulish details of such cases was lost on her, and the older she got the less she understood it. "We give them nothing but the basic facts. Have you all got that?" She looked at the heads, all nodding in unison. "I hope so. The less that gets out into the public domain at this stage, the better. Give them the whole story and we could have copycat killings on our hands, plus the usual crackpots who'll come forward and say they killed her."

"Those woods appear to be the killer's favourite location, ma'am," Hawkes said. "Shouldn't we be watching them?"

"It's not too big an area but there are multiple ways in and out. But you're right, despite the killer no doubt knowing what we've found by now, a police presence will do no harm." She nodded at one of the uniforms. "The cottages up there are owned by the water company who maintain the nearby reservoir. Some of their operatives live in them. Find out if anyone's got a spare room so two of you can stay there and keep watch."

A uniformed officer called DC Tony Birch put up his hand. "Some of them are empty, ma'am. I'll speak to the water board about us having one of those."

"We'll keep it in mind," Alice said, wondering if it was worth the trouble. The killer must know those cottages were there and would be wary of being watched. "But giving the girl a name is of prime importance. There's a family somewhere and they should know what's happened to her. I'm relying on you all to find that out quickly, so don't let me down."

Initial chat over, Alice returned to her office, put the case file on her desk, grabbed her coat and went to join Hawkes. "We should be off. Dolly will be wanting to start."

"Let's hope she gives us something," he said. "This latest body is all we've got to work with. Whoever is behind these killings knows what he's doing. If the girl hadn't been found so sharpish we'd be back at square one."

19

"He's slipped up, didn't bury the girl deep enough. Was that a mistake or deliberate?" she said.

"You think the killer is playing with us?"

"I'm not sure. We've met killers before who know how to yank our strings, Sergeant — or have you forgotten?"

"Still Waters," he said at once. "No, ma'am, I haven't forgotten, but at least then we knew who the victims were. There are three bodies already in the morgue with no names, and now this one."

"And possibly those we've not found yet," she added. "I trust Dolly. She will do her level best to find us something we can work with. We find out who the girl is and we're up and running."

"Have you given any thought to the killer's motive, ma'am?"

"Yes, Hawkes, these last few days I've thought of little else. It boils down to two possibilities. One, he's not fussy and chooses his victims at random, which will make things tricky for us. But they are all of a similar age, so I'm tending to disregard that one. The second is that he knows them all from somewhere and is seeking revenge because of an incident in the past. Until we have at least one identity, it'll be impossible to decide which is which."

Hawkes frowned. "Hmm. Some historic incident that's made him vengeful. Could be. Like you say, the girls who've already been found are of an age. It could be drug related."

Alice had also thought of that one. "True, it might. But if the killings are random, he might just be some nutter with a thing for teenage girls."

CHAPTER FOUR

Tuesday

Andrew Hewson paced the hallway with growing irritation. "Maggie! You've got ten seconds and then I'm gone."

He heard his daughter swear. Then she appeared on the landing at the top of the stairs. "You'll just have to wait. I can't find my homework and Mr Davies will kill me. He won't listen, he'll just assume I didn't bother doing it."

More often than not, Mr Davies would be right too. Maggie had let her schoolwork slip lately. She was too wrapped up in that waste-of-space boyfriend of hers, Freddie something or other. More times than he could count, she couldn't get up in the morning because she'd been up half the night chatting with him on her phone. "I can't wait any longer. I've got an appointment and I'm late already. You'll have to make your own way to school."

She leaned over the banister and glared down at him. "No time for me as usual. Well, don't you worry, I'll catch the bus and get knocked about by them scrotes from the estate."

It was six months since his wife walked out on them, a new man in tow. Was he coping? Not even close. Andrew

Hewson found life with his teenage daughter difficult, to say the least. He was endlessly conflicted about the best way to handle Maggie. Should he try to make a friend of his daughter? Be harder on her? His wife had always been the one to cope and he'd left her to it.

He'd never appreciated what a first class pain Maggie could be but it certainly hit home this morning. He'd hoped for a slow start to the day and a clear head. What he got was an angry teenage girl determined to make his life difficult.

Hewson had an important meeting with a supplier in Rochdale and his career hinged on the outcome. Get it right and there was a bonus and possible promotion in it. Get it wrong and it would be his job.

Kendrick's Textiles, a bedding manufacturer and long-standing customer was getting the boot. Smallshaws Soft Furnishings, the chain of shops Hewson worked for as a buyer, could no longer afford to use them. Going completely against the current trend and its demand for the cheap and cheerful, Kendrick's owner was determined to continue producing goods of high quality and had thereby priced them out of the market. Smallshaws couldn't afford to stock them anymore, and their customers certainly couldn't afford to buy them.

"I'm off. Make sure you lock up properly and set the alarm," Hewson barked up the stairs and marched out, slamming the front door shut behind him.

Maggie was a problem but he was equally wound up about the meeting with Ralph Kendrick. This was the third local manufacturer he'd given the chop to this month. Smallshaws was buying from a foreign firm now. They were cheaper and offered fast delivery, and that was all that mattered to Hewson's manager. But his manager didn't do the dirty work, he did.

When Hewson had the time, he fully intended to take Maggie in hand. Lay down the ground rules, meet and vet the boyfriend. All he'd seen of him so far was a fleeting glimpse. He needed to get to know the lad, understand what made him tick. This Freddie bloke was fast taking control of Maggie's life and she no longer listened to him. She stayed out late, drinking mostly, and last week he'd found the remnants of a spliff in her room. He'd tackled her and got a mouthful of abuse for his trouble. This would never have happened when her mother was still with them.

Ava was a hard woman who didn't stand any nonsense, so when she'd been around, Maggie towed the line. But Ava had her new life and her new man down south. Since she'd left, Maggie had run wild and Hewson was unable to control her. He was way out of his depth. He'd always left the child-rearing to Ava while he'd pursued his career and earned the money. He'd always considered it to be an arrangement that worked well. How wrong he'd been.

The man who'd whisked Ava away to a so called 'better life' didn't do kids and he particularly did not do teenage girls. Hewson couldn't get his head round it. How could a mother simply walk out and leave her child behind? Climbing into his car, he glanced back at the house. Maggie was standing at her bedroom window, her face glued to her mobile again, laughing and chatting as if she had nothing better to do.

What was the use. There was no way he'd win this one.

The Hewson's home was a three-bed semi in the better side of Droylsden, on the outskirts of Manchester. It was handy for the office in town but the ride out to Rochdale was something he could do without, particularly today. He had Kendrick's to sort and then he had a manufacturer to see in Glossop. He knew before he even left his driveway that he'd be spending most of the day stuck in traffic, particularly over Mottram moor on his second call. All this on top of his domestic problems.

* * *

Kendrick's Textiles was a family firm that hadn't moved with the times. The cutting machinery in the factory was old, the machinists were good and the quality of the goods excellent but they would do a quicker job if they had modern equipment to work with — Hewson knew very well that the sewing machines regularly broke down. Ralph Kendrick and his brother, Felix, employed a workforce of twenty but there were often five or six of them sitting idle because their machines were faulty.

Grabbing his briefcase from the boot of his car, he made his way to the office. It was a cluttered, ill-lit space full of old furniture. As always, Ralph Kendrick, a man in his mid sixties, was seated behind his desk, his head in a dogeared accounts ledger that looked as if it'd come out of the rk. His brother was nowhere to be seen.

"You've read my email?" Hewson began.

Kendrick shook his head. "I leave the technical stuff to Felix or Rhona, the office girl. I haven't got time for all that, and both of them have been off all week." He looked up. "D'you want a cup of tea?"

The email had been a waste of time then, which was a pity because he had written it to pave the way for the difficult conversation to come. "No thanks, busy morning. You work too hard, Ralph. Have you considered computerising the office systems? What's that you're doing, double entry bookkeeping? A decent software package could do the lot in a fraction of the time."

"Like I said, I don't get on with all that modern stuff. We've been using this method since my grandfather's time, and it works fine. I do the books, hand them to my accountant and he does the rest."

Hewson sat down opposite him at the desk. "I need to tell you something, and I'm afraid you're not going to like it."

Kendrick looked up, his tired grey eyes suddenly quizzical.

"It's the way you work, Ralph, your office systems, and that factory next door. You're lagging way behind the times. You can't meet your production targets anymore — in short, you simply can't compete. It's a cutthroat market out there, you know."

Kendrick's face turned red. "Everyone knows the Kendrick name. We offer quality. Our cloth is the finest Egyptian cotton, not the shoddy stuff being shipped in from the Far East. My girls work hard, they get the orders out. In all these years, we've never let you down."

Hewson nodded. "That's true, after a fashion, Ralph, but cost is everything. If Smallshaws were to keep you on we'd need a much shorter turnaround time and a sizeable price cut."

"We can't work any faster than we do already. My girls are good, they do first-class work. I ask them to cut corners and they won't understand." He shook his head. "It can't be done, Andrew. Not by me, not by any firm I can name."

"Yes it can, Ralph," Hewson said firmly. "Smallshaws are buying made up goods from the Far East because they are half the price and the quality is good enough for the customers. Firms like yours belong to a different age. I've warned you often enough. Things should have changed a long time ago for Kendrick's to make it in the current climate."

Ralph Kendrick put his hands down on the desk. "So that's it then? Just like that. One email and a visit so swift you haven't even got time for a cup of tea. We've supplied your shops for twenty years and now it's over, all because that boss of yours wants to line his pockets."

"It's not just that, Ralph. We have to change how we operate, or we go under too. It's a different world today and firms like yours just don't belong."

Ralph Kendrick stared at him for several seconds, an inscrutable expression across his face. "And what about my staff? What are they going to say? I'll have to sack the bloody lot of them. God knows what it'll do to our Felix. He's not well as it is. This news will finish him." He closed the ledger and tossed it across the desk. "Do you realise what you've done?"

Hewson got to his feet. This was about to get messy. "Look, I'm sorry that your brother will be upset. Talk to him, see if there is something the pair of you can come up with to make Kendrick's more competitive."

Ralph Kendrick's expression was stony. The set of his jaw told Hewson the idea didn't appeal. "I'll settle the outstanding account before the end of the month. Make sure that boss of yours knows that this is the end of Kendrick's Textiles. We're finished as a company. He's a first-class swine and you're no better. You'll get your comeuppance, the pair of you. You should have told me weeks ago that this was coming."

"I tried," Hewson said. "I've told you before about modernising the factory but you don't listen."

"Sod off. Go on, get out of my sight, and don't bother coming back. I wouldn't trade with Smallshaws now if you begged me."

CHAPTER FIVE

Dr Dolly Parkes had the girl's body laid out on the slab. She'd made the major incisions, removed the internal organs and was ready to go. She looked up at the viewing platform and nodded at the detectives.

"I've made all the preliminary investigations. A teenage female, no older than sixteen or seventeen, and she's never been pregnant. As I told you previously, the cause of death was a slash to the throat that severed the carotid artery. I've done the X-rays and examined the internal organs. What I can tell you today is that during her short life she'd suffered several broken bones." She pointed to the right arm. "The ulna here, several ribs and the right clavicle have all been fractured at some point. I would say the fractures occurred in childhood, as they've long since healed. An accident, a fall down stairs, who knows. There is evidence that the ulna was never set, which is odd. Whoever was looking after her must have been aware of the injury but did nothing about it. She'd have been in a great deal of pain for some time and I don't understand why she wasn't taken to hospital. Due to it not being treated, the bone did not knit together properly and has left a large scar." She pointed again.

"The injury could have been the result of a beating," Alice suggested. "If it was inflicted by a parent, they'd probably do their best to hide what was going on."

"Exactly my thoughts." Dolly's expression darkened with anger. "When you find her parents be sure to ask them for me. Anyway, getting back to the job in hand, there are marks on her legs and body which suggest a recent beating. The bruises are fairly new. The girl is underweight and short for her age, I've taken blood samples and will run the usual tests plus ones for malnutrition."

"Does that mean she was starved while she was being held captive?" Hawkes asked.

"Her stomach contents weren't up to much — what I'd describe as a watery porridge, that was all. But she could have been living rough on the streets before she was taken. That would also account for her poor physical condition. We'll see what the blood results throw up. I've taken prints but there is no match on the database. We'll do our best to repair the front teeth and mouth so she looks reasonably presentable."

"How long will that take?" Alice asked. "I'm anxious to get photos of her out there. Catching this killer hinges on finding the identity of his victims, and currently she's our best bet."

Dolly smiled at her. "It won't take long. We don't intend to do anything too technical — a bit of modelling clay and make-up can work wonders. I'll have her looking decent in case you find a family member who wants to see her. As for her name, you don't need to wait for someone to recognise her from the photo and come forward. I can tell you right now who she is."

This was brilliant news. "Really? How come? You don't recognise her from somewhere, do you?"

Dolly shook her head. "This was one clever girl. Knowing that she was about to be killed, she had the presence of mind to let whoever found her know who she was. As we know, she was found wearing a white, hand-stitched shroud, and from the untidy stitching it looks like needlework was not her thing. Plus, I suspect she was at the task for a while, spinning out what little time she had left. Whoever was holding her can't have checked her work or they'd have discovered what she was up to. She turned up a generous hem at the bottom and embroidered her name on the inside of it in white cotton. I might have missed it but the dirt on the shroud highlighted the letters. She added the name of another girl who was probably imprisoned with her."

Alice was flabbergasted. Imagine. So young and facing death, yet she'd thought of that.

"Her name is Ellie Fleming," Dolly said. "As for the other girl we only have her first name, Josie."

"She didn't leave us the name of her killer, did she by any chance?" Alice asked hopefully.

"Not as far as I can see. But that part of the hem has rotted away from being in the damp soil. And there's not much left of the stitching."

Shame, but at least they had the victim's name. "Go and ring the team back at the station and tell them what we've got," Alice told Hawkes.

"Jack will give the garment another good going over to make sure we haven't missed anything. He still has one or two tests up his sleeve. I'll call as soon as the results come in, tomorrow at the latest."

"Knowing if she'd been on drugs might help," Alice said. "Also, anything at all on the body or that shroud that could tell us where she'd been imprisoned or where she was living before that."

"From the state of her she might well have been a rough sleeper but we shouldn't jump to that conclusion," Dolly said. "Her fingernails are bitten to the quick and there's dirt ingrained in her body like you see in homeless people. But of course, a lot of it will have come from the grave. Alternatively, she might not have been able to wash while she was in captivity."

Poor girl. Alice's heart went out to her. She must often have been tempted to give in to despair. But she hadn't, Ellie had fought, she'd tried to stay alive for as long as she could and thought of the future. Alice truly admired this brave girl.

Minutes later, Jason Hawkes was back, a smile on his face. "We've got a hit, ma'am. An Ellie Fleming was reported missing by a concerned neighbour thirteen months ago."

"Not a parent?"

"No, ma'am, and that same neighbour had also contacted social services about the girl in the past."

"You have an address for our victim?"

Hawkes grimaced. "The Langdale estate in Ardwick."

Alice nodded. No wonder he'd made that face. The Langdale had spawned any number of villains over the years, and she was always on her guard whenever she had to pay it a visit.

"We'll take a couple of plainclothes guys to watch our backs," she said. "I know the Langdale of old and I bet it's no better these days."

"Half the dealers in Manchester ply their trade from that eyesore. The council should have ripped the place down years ago."

"You're right, Sergeant, I'm as uncomfortable about the place as you are."

Alice called down to Dolly that they were off.

"The initial report will be on the system later," Dolly said.

"Ring the station and get DC Barrow and a colleague to meet us," Alice said to Hawkes. "There's a pub called the Red Lion on the corner as you drive into the estate. Tell them we'll meet them in the car park."

"If she lived on the Langdale, I'm not surprised she got out as fast as she could. The killer may have offered her a way out and she took it. Most of the adults there have never done a day's work in their lives, and as far as the dealers are concerned it's more or less drug central," Hawkes muttered.

"The estate doesn't concern us right now, Hawkes. What we're interested in is Ellie's life, her family and any friends she had there. If she grew up in the place, it wouldn't have felt as scary to her as it does to us. I also want to know why it was down to a 'concerned neighbour' to report Ellie missing. What about her parents?"

"I doubt she had any, ma'am. Well, not a father anyway. Most of the kids in that estate are dragged up. They're drug runners by the age of ten, with worse to follow."

"There must have been a mother somewhere. Wasn't she worried about Ellie's welfare? She was a young teenage girl for goodness sake. And what about school?" Alice said.

"The kids from there go to Ardwick High. It's actually a pretty good school. If Ellie was continually absent, her mother would have got real grief from them," Hawkes said.

"It would help us if her mother is still around to interview, and especially that neighbour. She'll be worth talking to."

CHAPTER SIX

Ellie's mother's house was at the end of a block of ten town-houses that had been built back in the sixties. The house was a shambles. The gable end had received the close attention of the local youth, who'd daubed gang tags all over it, while the front garden looked like it was used as the estate rubbish tip. There was no gate, the wooden fence had been ripped up and left lying on what had been a lawn in some distant past. The pair picked their way gingerly through broken glass and empty beer cans to the front door.

"Look at it. Not seen a brush in months." Hawkes tutted.

Alice banged on the front door and waited. "The rest of the street is the same. There was talk of this part of the estate being demolished — the cement is all wrong, it's rotting or something." She nodded at a large empty area of ground several metres away. "There used to be a block of flats there until someone spotted the rot and it was torn down."

He shook his head. "Yet people still live here."

"It would appear so. Mrs Fleming!" Alice called out. "We'd like a word."

They waited. Several minutes passed before finally the net curtain covering the grimy front window twitched.

"Nip round the back," Alice told Hawkes, "in case she tries to dodge us."

But she didn't. Before he could move, the front door opened. "You're police, aren't you? Found the little bitch comatose in some alley then, have you?"

The woman stood looking up at her, small, skinny and probably not yet forty. But she was old before her time. The lines already etched on her face were only emphasised by the hair, dyed a jet black, that hung, lank, around her shoulders. Alice gave her a smile. "You should invite me in, we don't want to alarm the neighbours, do we?"

The woman cast a glance up and down the street and stood aside. "I've done nowt, so don't start with the accusations. And it's Johnson now. I went back to my maiden name when that bastard Les ran out on us. Three weeks of marriage, that's all I got. Left me up the duff, and with a shed load of debt. I haven't seen him since." The small sitting room reeked of tobacco. She immediately lit a cigarette, took a long drag and blew out a plume of smoke which disappeared into the general miasma. "Not found him, have you? I've been praying for years that the useless lump would turn up dead somewhere."

"I've no idea where your husband is, Miss Johnson."

"The name's Gloria."

"I'm here about your daughter Ellie, not your husband."

At the sound of the name, Glora turned her back on Alice and, wreathed in smoke, stared out of the window. "He with you?"

"That's my sergeant, we'd better let him in."

"Your time would be better spent doing sommat else. Our Ellie's a waste of space. He might not have brought her up but she's got the worst of Les in her. I knew when she was small that the kid wouldn't amount to much. Too lippy, couldn't keep it shut and it was always getting her into trouble."

The woman hadn't asked anything about her daughter — whether she was well, where she was, or even if she was alive.

33

Nothing. Not much more than sixteen and her mother didn't give a damn. "We believe your daughter is dead, Gloria," Alice said with as much sympathy as she could muster. "We've found a body and are running tests to verify that it is Ellie. It would help if you'd give a DNA sample so we can confirm it."

Gloria Johnson pulled on her cigarette. "No need, love. My prints and DNA are already on record. Three years ago — soliciting. Piccadilly bus station in th'town centre. I mouthed off at a copper that night, thumped him too, so I got arrested."

"Were you using your own name?" Alice asked.

Gloria nodded.

Alice caught Hawkes rolling his eyes and shot him a warning look. They weren't here to criticise how Ellie's mother chose to keep body and soul together. They needed information and getting that depended on not rocking the boat. "When did you last see Ellie?"

"She don't live here but she comes back every so often. The last time was about six month ago."

"Was she okay? Did she look well?"

"Not really. She'd been on the juice as well as the drugs."

"Did she say what her plans were?" Alice asked.

"Plans? Ellie? She's not organised enough for plans, love. Last time she came round she did a runner with my benefit money, thieving bitch."

"It'd help to know the names and addresses of any friends Ellie had," Alice said.

"Friends? She wasn't the type to have friends. Ellie latched onto folk. She used them and then ditched 'em once she'd wrung 'em dry." She blew smoke in Alice's direction, which made her gag. "Mind you, there were that gang she hung around with before she took off. Five of 'em there were, including Ellie. All as bad as each other, thick as thieves for a while. Always up to mischief."

"Did she ever mention a girl called Josie?" Alice asked.

Gloria shook her head. "Not to me she didn't. The only one I remember is Louise Morley. Louise's granny is half decent and it surprised me when I found out she was involved with our Ellie. Mind you, she had poor taste in men. Louise went out with that hoodlum pal of Laser's for a while." Gloria shook her head. "Doesn't surprise me that our Ellie ended up dead. That gob of hers was always going to do for her. Cross some dealer, did she?"

"We're still investigating."

"Stupid cow," Gloria said, flicking ash onto the floor. "Didn't mind who she mixed with — estate lads, city lads, anyone who'd stand her a fix. She was working for that Laser and his predecessor for a while. What, you don't know Laser? He runs one of them county lines. You should have a word."

"Does he have a name?"

"Laser."

"I mean his real name," Alice said.

"Laser's all I've got. You'll have seen his tag on th'house. Matter of fact it's all over the estate. Find him. Ask him what happened to Ellie. You're wasting your time asking me."

Sad but true. Ellie's own mother, and she hadn't a clue about the girl's life these last few years. "How old would she have been?"

"Seventeen in a month. She left 'ere when she were fourteen, and has hardly been back since."

"Did you see her around the estate after she left home?"

"No. She kept her head down and I didn't go looking. I heard she'd split with Laser, so I reckon she moved away."

Ellie's mother spoke as if she were discussing a stranger, not the child she'd given birth to.

"Ellie sustained several broken bones when she was a child. A neighbour reported her concerns to social services. What d'you know about that?" Alice asked.

"That'll be the cow from number ten. Never could keep her nose out. She thought Ellie was treated badly and mouthed off about it to anyone who'd listen."

"Does she still live there?" Alice asked.

"No, she died last year. Good riddance, that's what I say. I got no time for do-gooders, especially them who go in for reporting folk to the social."

Disappointed at this news, Alice handed Gloria a card. "My number, in case anything else occurs to you."

"What about burying her and all that? I don't have any money, so it'll have to be a cheap do."

"We're a way off that yet, Gloria," Alice said.

CHAPTER SEVEN

Hawkes waited until they were back in the car before bursting out. "That woman has no shame."

"Living on the breadline, a challenging family and no support. I don't condone her actions, Sergeant, but I do understand what led to them. Gloria Johnson is no different to hundreds of other women in this city. Life can be unforgiving, never forget that."

"Even so, the kid was so young. All she needed was someone to guide her and show her some love."

He was right, but they didn't live in a perfect world and neither he nor she could change it. "We'll return to the station, check the records and make sure Gloria was telling the truth. Once we have her DNA we'll get Jack Nevin to check for a familial match."

"What about this Laser person?" Hawkes asked.

"I'll ask the local police. If he's a dealer, they'll know all about him."

Alice checked her watch, it was gone five in the afternoon. She was looking forward to a strong coffee and a bite to eat. But that would have to wait. She arrived at the station to find an argument raging in the reception area. Ordinarily, Alice would pass by without interfering, but she happened to hear something the irate visitor was saying, and it set alarm bells ringing.

"When are you going to do something about it? My daughter's been missing since this morning. She didn't go to school and none of her friends have seen her. There's been no calls, no message and she hasn't posted anything on social media. She's sixteen for God's sake. Tell me, when does that happen with someone her age?"

Alice stopped in her tracks. Telling Hawkes to go ahead, she went to speak to the man.

"I'll deal with this," she told the uniformed PC behind the counter, and turned to the anxious parent. "I'm DCI Alice Rossi. How can I help?"

"Andrew Hewson," he responded. "I'm going out of my mind with worry. Maggie has never done anything like this before. I've visited all her usual haunts and spoken to her friends and the school, but she's nowhere to be found."

Alice ushered him towards an interview room. "I'll take some details from you, if I may."

"This'll be my fault," he continued. "She'll be sulking. Maggie and I had words this morning. I was late for a meeting and couldn't wait for her so I didn't drop her at school as I usually do. I returned earlier than normal to sort something to eat, to find an empty house and no sign of Maggie. No school bag, no sign of her having eaten. Nothing. She finishes school at twelve today so my first thought was that she'd gone off somewhere with her friends. I rang her mobile but it was either turned off or had run out of battery. That's not like Maggie at all — the thing is almost always glued to her face. Then I rang round her friends, of whom there's a fair few I can tell you. All of them told me they hadn't seen her today. Instinctively I felt that something was wrong so my next stop was you lot."

"Is there any chance that Maggie could have run away? Could she be staying with a friend or relative who might not tell you where she is?"

"I suppose anything's possible. She was really pissed off with me this morning. The problem is, as far as I can tell, she hasn't taken any of her clothes. She's got her mobile certainly, and I know she keeps cash stashed in a tin under her bed and that's gone too. But it's the social media thing — she's posted nothing, and even if she had done a runner, I know she couldn't resist putting something up."

"Do you have a recent photo of her?" Alice asked.

Hewson had come prepared. He reached in his inside jacket pocket and handed it over. "Taken two weekends ago at a friend's barbecue."

"Does she have a special friend, someone she confides in or might go and stay with?"

"Yes. Gemma Roberts, but I've rung her. I told her I was coming here and made a point of telling her she had to let me know if she hears anything about Maggie. I left Gemma under no illusion as to how worried I am."

Fair enough. Alice could only hope that the girl appreciated his concern. "I also need her mobile phone number. I will contact her provider and get them to forward the data from it."

"Will that help?"

"It might. We'll know who Maggie called, who called her, any text she sent and received and her social media activity. There may be people she contacts that you don't know about."

Hewson didn't look any less anxious. "Look, I know the score, I've seen the news and heard about those other missing girls. I'm continually telling Maggie to be careful, to watch where she goes and the people around her."

Alice understood where he was coming from. "There's unlikely to be any connection. But our patrol cars will keep a look out for her and if we hear anything at all, one of my team will be in touch. You haven't mentioned Maggie's mother. Does she live with you?"

"No, she lives down south. I've rung her, so she knows what's happened. If Maggie turns up at hers, she'll tell me."

"Nonetheless, I'd like her address." She gave the man a reassuring smile. "Chances are Maggie will calm down, see sense and come home before long."

"I hope so, I won't sleep until she's home. The thing is, it's so unlike her. We argue, of course, she's a teenage girl, but she's never done anything like this before."

"Does Maggie have a boyfriend?" Alice asked.

"Yes. His name's Freddie Whitton, he's older than Maggie and is no longer at school. He's got a job and his own flat that he shares with mates, but that's all I know about him."

"If I were you, I'd go home in case she rings or turns up. I'm sure all will be well. Leave Gemma and Freddie's addresses with the sergeant on the desk and we'll get an officer to go round. If Maggie is staying with one of them, I'm sure she'll see sense. When she finally does come home, let me know," Alice said handing him her card.

"You're a DCI, I see. How come you're interested in this? It's not something you'd normally concern yourself with, is it?"

Hewson was thinking about the missing teenagers. "I happened to overhear what you were saying to the sergeant in reception and I decided to have a word myself. Try not to worry too much, she's probably just being a teenager. However, if she hasn't turned up by this time tomorrow, we'll put out an appeal on the local news."

"So, you are linking her disappearance to those of the other girls," he said.

"Not at all but I wouldn't be doing my job if I didn't take your worries seriously, particularly in view of what has happened recently."

This seemed to appease Hewson but Alice knew he must be frantic with worry. Why had his daughter done this? Surely that morning's spat hadn't been serious enough to make her run away. But then it was a long time since Alice had been a teenager.

CHAPTER EIGHT

"That was an interesting one." Alice was back in the incident room, talking to Hawkes. "I've just spoken to a father whose teenage daughter has gone walkabout. Uniform have the details and will start making enquiries, but it'll do no harm for us to keep our eyes and ears open as well."

She wrote the names 'Maggie Hewson' and 'Freddie Whitton' on the incident board and pinned up a copy of the photo of Maggie.

"D'you think she's fallen victim to our killer, ma'am?" Roger Wallis asked, indicating the image of Maggie Hewson on the board.

"As you can see, she fits the profile but we're a long way from that. I want you to get all her mobile phone data. We need to know what Maggie was up to before she ran away."

Alice turned and addressed the team. "The good news is that we have a name for the most recent victim found in Ravenswood. She was called Ellie Fleming, seventeen years old, from the Langdale estate. She ran away at fourteen and has only been back home for the occasional visit since then." She picked up a board marker. "Okay. People of interest in the case: an individual with the street name 'Laser', who's a small-time dealer that Ellie hung out with. He may not be of much use but since he was a boyfriend of sorts, he might be able to tell us something. Speak to Uniform and the drug squad and have him brought in. Also, try and find out what happened to her father, Les Fleming. You might have to cast the net wide on that one."

"Those woods where the girls were buried don't cover a large area but it's still easy to get lost in them," Roger Wallis said. "DC Barrow and I have been up there for a look around. Apart from the cottages there are no other buildings that we can see. The graves are some distance from anywhere you can park a vehicle, so the bodies must have been carried or transported some other way to the burial place. Given that the place is popular with dog walkers, I think we can go with the hypothesis that the killer must have moved the bodies after dark, and therefore knows the area well."

Alice nodded. Sounded reasonable.

"There is one thing that I did note," Wallis said. "There's a textile factory — Kendrick's — at the end of one of the paths that leads into the woods. The building is two or three storeys high so it must look out over the woods."

"Good work," Alice said. "That'll need checking out. Meanwhile, get out to the Langdale and find this Laser character. He's known to us, so speak to Uniform and try his usual haunts."

Alice looked at the map of Ravenswood pinned on the wall. Each grave was marked on it. The killer had chosen a spot under the trees in more or less the centre of the woodland. "There's still a few hours before it goes dark. I'd like to take a look at Kendrick's factory building for myself," she told Hawkes. "You and me shortly, all right?"

* * *

Ravenswood was no less eerie than on Alice's first visit. It was sunny today, too, but the late summer warmth made little difference to the air of menace. But Hawkes needed to see for himself where the bodies had been found, so show him she must. Then, as Alice looked around, she suddenly realised why she felt so spooked. The sound of water and the upward sweep of the hills in the distance were just like Still Waters.

"Kendrick's is that way." She pointed. "We'll have a word with whoever is in charge and weigh up the workforce. Apart from the water board cottages over there it's the only building around. Have the cottages been looked at?"

"The ones that are occupied," Hawkes said. "According to Birch, no one objected to him having a poke around and they were all happy to answer questions. But we'll need to get keys for the empty ones from the water board. You never know, someone might have got in without permission."

"See to it that you go over every inch, and make sure the cellars and attics are thoroughly checked," Alice said.

"Birch is thorough, ma'am."

They went back to the car and drove the short distance to Kendrick's. The old Victorian stone building was badly in need of repair. The paint on the doors was peeling and there was even a window frame hanging loose on the top floor. Given Kendrick's reputation for quality, Alice was surprised at how run-down it was.

The inside was no better. Alice felt as if she'd stepped back in time as she gazed across row upon row of women working at sewing machines. The space was cold and had plenty of trip hazards. "The factory inspector would have a field day with this place," she whispered. "The equipment is positively antique."

Halfway across the workroom they were approached by a stern-looking, middle-aged woman in a dark suit. "If you're here to see Mr Felix, I'm afraid he's off sick. Mr Ralph might see you but he's a busy man. It would have been prudent to make an appointment."

Alice held up her warrant card. "As a police officer, I had no need to make an appointment. Now go and tell him we're here and not to keep us waiting."

The woman huffed. "Can I tell him what it's about?"

"Murder." Alice kept her voice low, not wanting to upset any of the workers.

As the woman scuttled off, Alice heard a few giggles from the seamstresses. No doubt it was very satisfying to see the old harridan put in her place.

Working in this old-fashioned, inhospitable place must be soul destroying. Alice wondered why these women did it.

"You from the insurance company?" one of them asked. "Is this about the accident?"

"No, we're here about something else," Hawkes said.

"What accident?" Alice asked.

"Eliza got her hand caught in the cutting machine a couple of weeks ago. Ten stitches it needed and she's not been able to work since. She says she's had no choice but to make a claim. All she's got is state sick pay, this place has given her nowt, so the poor girl's on the breadline."

Alice could well imagine the accidents working with equipment as old as this would incur.

The stern woman reappeared and gestured towards a door at the far end of the factory. "Mr Kendrick will see you now."

"What's the betting he looks like he's just stepped out of a Dickens novel," Hawkes whispered. "I'd no idea places like this still existed."

"Me neither, Sergeant."

CHAPTER NINE

Ralph Kendrick did indeed look like something out of Dickens. He was in his sixties but with his white hair and old-fashioned tweed suit, he looked much older. He was seated at a large oak desk with a battered old ledger open in front of him, busy working on an antiquated adding machine.

"What have we done to attract the attention of the police?" he asked. "Mrs Hubble says you mentioned murder. Surely neither I nor my brother are suspects?"

While he spoke, Alice was gazing out of the office window. From here there was a good view right across Ravenswood, including the tops of the trees where the bodies had been found.

"The bodies of four young women have been found down there." She pointed. "And now I'm here I can see the scene is visible from your office window."

"I wouldn't know. Bad eyesight. I'm waiting for a cataract operation in both eyes, so my distance vision is limited." He showed her a magnifying glass that had been on the desk beside him. "I use this for close work since my glasses are no longer strong enough. Fortunately my distance vision is considerably better. The short sightedness came with the cataract surgery I had."

Seeing the way he squinted at the figures on the page, Alice believed him. "You employ mostly female staff. Do they stay in the job for long?"

"Yes, most of them stay a good while. Why d'you ask?"

"The murder victims were all young females, teenagers."

Kendrick shook his head. "We don't employ anyone that young. Twenty-five years of age at least, when they've got some sense. And we do like them to have some previous experience on the machines."

"Has the firm been here long?" Hawkes asked.

"Yes, almost a century, but we won't be here much longer." He said this bitterly.

"Problems?"

"Smallshaws, our sole distributer in the North West, has dropped us. Unless they change their minds it's the end for Kendrick's, although I don't know what we can do to make them see sense. They say we're old fashioned, can't compete in today's market."

From what she'd seen, Alice reckoned Smallshaws had a point but she said nothing.

"They've no idea what they're talking about," Kendrick continued. "Quality doesn't go out of fashion, and that's exactly what we produce, nothing more, nothing less."

"What exactly do you produce here if I may ask?" said Hawkes.

"We import the finest Egyptian cotton, weave it into cloth and make it into bedsheets." He smiled. "It's a real skill. Our girls go through a period of intensive training and then when they're ready they move onto the factory floor. As for the cloth itself, we have a number of skilled weavers who work in a building behind this one. They're a dying breed, believe me. We do our best to turn out first-class goods, but Smallshaws still aren't happy. They tell me we're too slow and too expensive, so they've gone elsewhere and are buying foreign rubbish. The problem is, the public are so ignorant that they're buying it."

He heaved a deep sign and threw his pen onto the desk. "What's the use. This place will close down by the end of the month. Smallshaws have done for us, and there's nothing we can do."

"I'm sorry to hear that," Alice said. "It's a tough world out there, I'm afraid. It's match the competition or go under."

"I will retire and my brother, Felix, will have to make his own way in the world. The people I feel most sorry for are those women out there. They'll have a hard time finding alternative work around here. Smallshaws have no idea what they've done. Still, it's just a matter of time before they come unstuck too. Like that idiot Hewson told me, this business is cut-throat."

Alice's ears pricked up. "Andrew Hewson?"

"Yes, he's our rep from Smallshaws. He was here earlier. Told me we were finished and buggered off to ruin someone else's day."

Alice looked at Hawkes. She'd no idea what this meant. Was it significant in some way, or just one huge coincidence? But whatever it meant, Andrew Hewson, whose own daughter was now missing, knew this area. She looked more carefully at Ralph Kendrick. Could he have taken the girl to get his own back? No. Look at the man. He was old before his time and obviously far from strong. But he did have a brother, and the sooner they spoke to him the better.

"We will have to speak to your staff and your brother as soon as possible. We need to ask them if they've seen anything or anyone out there in the woods. I'll send a colleague round to arrange that."

"Do as you please," Kendrick said.

"You've been very helpful, Mr Kendrick." She handed him her card. "If anything occurs to you, please give me a ring."

* * *

"That was weird," Hawkes said, once they were back in the car. "Fancy that man Hewson knowing this place."

"We'll be sure to ask him about it," Alice said. "It might be important or it might not. But I'll give it some thought

47

before diving in. He came to us, remember. And he's genuinely worried sick about his daughter."

"D'you reckon there's anyone in that place who could be a suspect?" Hawkes asked. "The owner struck me as a strange one, old-fashioned, thin and bony. Not someone I'd like to meet on a dark night for sure. The women seemed tame enough though."

Alice smiled at him. "He's old before his time and stuck in his ways, we can hardly charge him with that. We will speak to the brother though. In fact, do that when we get back to the station. Give him a call and make an appointment. You and Roger Wallis can organise interviews with the staff too. Some of those women might use the paths through the woods as a shortcut. You never know, one of them could have seen something and not realised."

"Back to the station, ma'am?"

"Yes, then I'm getting off home and I advise you to do the same. These next few days are going to be full on."

CHAPTER TEN

Wednesday

Alice had had better starts to her day. She'd hurried downstairs to make herself a cup of coffee but when she plugged in the kettle, the thing blew up on her.

"Came out of the Ark, that did." Dilys was just letting herself in by the back door when it happened. "Go and finish getting ready and I'll boil some water in a pan for your coffee."

"I'll pick up a new kettle at lunchtime," Alice decided. "That's the trouble with this house, it and everything in it are as old as the hills."

"It was good enough for your parents," Dilys said. "And don't you forget it."

"Sorry. I've been awake half the night mulling over my latest case. It's one of those that's got us running around like headless chickens."

"You'll sort it out," Dilys said with confidence. "Otherwise, that superintendent of yours wouldn't have taken you on."

Alice smiled to herself. The reality was that the bigwig superintendent had given her Dream Catcher solely on the strength of the Still Waters case. Her success with that had given Leo Monk a way out of the stalemate he'd got himself into with Operation Dream Catcher.

While Dilys made coffee and toast, Alice went to get dressed. The bit that really puzzled her was motive. Apart from Ellie, the only thing they knew about the victims were that they were all of a similar age. Did they know each other? Come from the same sort of background? What had they all been mixed up in that had got them killed? As yet, it was nothing but supposition.

Dilys called up the stairs. "Your phone's ringing. It's that young detective, Jason."

Alice took the phone from her. "What've you got?"

"Laser, ma'am. He was picked up earlier this morning, dossing down in Piccadilly Gardens. He's in the cells awaiting interview."

"Has he said anything? Does he admit to knowing Ellie?"

"Admits to nothing. Young scally's got a mouth on him too. Reckons he's going to sue the lot of us for unlawful arrest."

"Give me thirty minutes and I'll be with you."

Alice finished the call and looked up to find Dilys holding out a tray with her breakfast on it. "Go on, get it down you. It might be the only thing you get to eat today."

True. Stuffing a slice of toast into her mouth, Alice went into the back room to get her notes and case files. "I'll be late back, so don't bother about dinner."

* * *

"What's he like, this Laser person? And have you got a proper name out of him yet?" Alice asked.

"Liam Lazelle, hence the nickname. And he's full of himself," Hawkes said. "You know the type — done nothing, knows nothing, and we've got it all wrong."

Alice looked at the sheet he handed to her. "Lazelle. Odd name, it doesn't sound local. Do we know where he's from?"

"I don't think he knows where he's from himself, or much else right now. He's taken something and needs to sleep it off."

"Shame, I was hoping to get this interview started." She ran her eyes down the sheet. "He's been arrested enough times, mostly for possession. Although not dealing, I see."

"Knows how to play it," Hawkes said. "He's probably got the bulk of his stuff stashed somewhere."

"Or in this instance, swallowed the lot," she said. "Does he have an address?"

"Not that we can get out of him. He just keeps raving on about police brutality and how he's going to sue us."

Alice shook her head. How many times had they had that one thrown at them? "Does he need to be in hospital?"

"No ma'am, strong coffee, a morning to sleep it off and he should be okay."

"All right, we'll attempt to have that chat this afternoon then." Alice walked into the incident room. The board was still woefully empty. They had four bodies, a name and little else. She added Liam Lazelle's name to the list and circled it. Currently, he was the closest they had to a person of interest.

"Who does this Laser hang out with?" she asked the team.

"Not sure, ma'am," Neil Barrow said. "He's seen on the Langdale often enough, the pub car park mostly, but he doesn't hang around."

"You see him with anyone?"

"Kids."

"Do we have any evidence that he's involved with one of the big dealers?" she asked.

Tony Birch checked his notes. "It says here that the prime mover in the Manchester drug world these days is thought to be Max Reagan. Recently he's spread his net wider, it's like a spider's web and his people are everywhere. Some of them are scarily young too."

"And the old guard?" Alice asked.

Birch shrugged. "Their noses shoved well out of joint."

"I don't expect they like someone moving into their patch."

"There's been surprisingly little in the way of trouble though, ma'am. It's very quiet out there, which is a bit of a surprise."

Alice had her own thoughts about that one. If the streets were quiet it meant that someone in the Manchester underbelly was ruling things with a rod of iron. Could it be this Reagan? Was he that powerful already?

Alice had another look at the board. Names, a couple of faces and word that the streets were quiet. Was this case really about drug dealing? It didn't sound like it.

"This Max Reagan, DC Birch, what do we know about him?"

"Not a lot, ma'am. He did a short stretch fifteen years ago for GBH. We know from the intel we've had that he is currently running the dealing in this city, but there's been no violence that we're aware of. He owns a fitness club down Oldham Road way. Spends most of his time there they say."

"Unusual. If there's little in the way of argument from anyone else, it looks like he has control. That isn't what usually happens, is it?" She studied the board deep in thought. "I think I'd like to meet this Reagan bloke. Meanwhile, team, I want everything you can find out about Ralph and Felix Kendrick."

CHAPTER ELEVEN

Alice was still staring at the board when DC Tony Birch called to her. "Dr Parkes is on the phone, ma'am."

Alice took the handset from him. Whatever she had been expecting, it wasn't what Dolly now told her.

"Jack has taken a closer look at the shroud the latest victim was wearing," Dolly began. "As we already know, it was stitched together from a bedsheet."

"Are we sure about that? Isn't one piece of white cotton cloth much like any other?" Alice said.

"This is very good quality cotton, but more important, we've found part of a Kendrick's label in the hem. I think Ellie was aware it might be important and has hidden it like she did her name."

"It's getting so I can't move without tripping over Kendrick's." But did it actually mean anything, she wondered. One way or another, it had to. Alice didn't believe in coincidence.

"The Kendrick's brand means the sheets were costly and not widely available. You might like to think about how and where our killer got hold of them. Meanwhile, Jack is taking another look at what's left of the shrouds the other girls were wearing. It's mostly rotted away but he reckons they're all made from the same fabric, Kendrick's Egyptian cotton."

That would take more than one sheet. "Thanks, Dolly, I'll look into it."

Call over, Alice updated the board and then turned to the team. "The shroud Ellie Fleming was wearing was made from a Kendrick's bedsheet. Forensics also think the other victims could well have been wearing ones made of the same fabric. We need to know where those sheets came from. Locally, the sole distributor of Kendrick's bedding is a firm called Smallshaws, who sell them online and through their stores, which you'll have seen in the retail parks. It might help to know how many of the sheets each store sells. Smallshaws are a large company with many outlets but Kendrick's stuff costs, so you might find that only certain stores sell it. You don't find bedding like that in the supermarkets. If it's possible, I'd like to find out where the bedsheet we found Ellie in came from. Unfortunately, that does mean taking a look at Smallshaws's stores, their customers as well as a closer look at the workforce at Kendrick's."

"DC Wallis, take a uniform and get back up there. Ask Ralph Kendrick if there is any pilfering and what they do with the stuff that doesn't turn out right — you know, the seconds. Find out when that brother of his will be available for interview, tell Kendrick it's urgent and start quizzing the staff. This time we come on strong. I want the full details of everyone who works in that factory. The garment the girl was buried in had one of their labels on it, there is no getting away from that. It might be a setup, someone unconnected to the factory may have deliberately chosen that particular fabric but we can't just assume that's the case. And given that their factory overlooks the burial site, I'm doubly suspicious that the place and the people in it are involved in some way."

Alice looked over at Hawkes, who was hanging onto her every word. "You and I will stay here and interview Lazelle when he comes round."

"And don't forget those empty cottages, DC Barrow. They too overlook the woods."

"If anyone was being kept in them," Barrow said dubiously, "the people in the other ones would have heard something, and they haven't. I've spoken to them all."

But Alice was firm. "We have more information now, Detective, and that changes things. I want them going over, just to make certain. It'll take you a day tops to go through the empty ones. Have you decided about using one of them?"

"The water board are sorting the paperwork, ma'am," he said, rather sulkily.

Alice nodded. "So have another word with the people living in the two that are occupied. Question them about Ellie Fleming. See if there is any reaction to the name."

"Kendrick's have got dozens of machinists," DC Wallis pointed out. "Speaking to them all will take a bit of time."

"Then compile a rota and split the interviews between you. Anyone whose answers you're not happy with, bring them in."

"What about Smallshaws?" Hawkes asked.

"Their agent was here yesterday." She pointed at the photo of Maggie Hewson on the board. "His daughter is missing, which is another coincidence I'm not happy with. I'll have another word with him myself later."

"D'you think he's hiding something, ma'am?" Hawkes asked.

"I'm not sure, but the fact that he's connected to that company is bugging me. He knows the Kendricks and is familiar with the place. We mustn't lose sight of that while we're looking for his daughter. If she hasn't turned up by four this afternoon, we'll get him in. We can do the appeal and have a chat afterwards."

"D'you think he's involved in the disappearance of the other girls?" DC Barrow asked.

"I don't know what to think." She grinned. "As things are, working this case is a bit like wading through mud."

"Ma'am." DC Tony Birch came into the room. "Lazelle is now fit to be interviewed. He's not feeling brilliant but he wants to get it over with."

Beckoning to Hawkes, Alice made for the door. Would Lazelle offer anything helpful? Alice doubted it. From what she'd been told, it sounded like he knew how to watch his back.

CHAPTER TWELVE

"You're wasting your time. I've got nowt to say."

The young man folded his arms, looking defiant.

"You don't know what we're going to ask you yet," Alice said.

"Bound to be bad, innit. Always is. Coppers drag me in, put me through the third degree then chuck me back on th'street. But while I'm here they throw the lot at me, all the outstanding stuff on the books, I reckon."

"We brought you in to ask you about a young girl called Ellie Fleming," Alice said.

At the sound of her name, Lazelle gave a start. "What about her?"

"She's dead, Liam. Ellie has been murdered."

"Call me Laser." Then it seemed to dawn on him and he stared. "Murdered? Why? Who did she cross?"

"We don't know that she crossed anyone. The fact is, we don't know anything about Ellie's life, which is why we're talking to you. But we do believe she was held a prisoner somewhere, along with some other girls who may or may not have been connected to her."

"Others? That's not like Ellie. She preferred her own company, except when she was on the streets. When she was living rough, she usually tagged onto a group. Safer like."

"When did you last see Ellie?" Hawkes asked.

Laser shrugged. "She dropped off the radar about two months ago and I haven't seen her since. But that's not unusual for her."

"Was she worried about anything? Getting grief from anyone?" Alice asked.

"Them letters were getting on her nerves. At least twice a week there was another one pushed under the door. She tried to catch the bugger who were leaving them but he was too quick."

"What letters?" Alice asked.

"Anonymous ones, threatening all sorts and not signed."

"Okay, from the beginning. Tell me everything you know about them."

"It was when she were living in a squat in Rusholme, an old student house long since left empty. That's when they started coming. They bothered her and I'm not surprised. She showed me a couple, poison they were. Whoever was sending them said he was going to take her prisoner and then kill her."

Which is exactly what happened. She glanced at Hawkes. He too looked grim. "Do you know what Ellie did with the letters?"

"She burnt them — most of them anyway," he said. "But there are still a few knocking around in her stuff."

"We could do with having a look at them," Alice said. "Is there anything more you can tell us about them?"

"Well, they were like written, not typed. Scratchy and old-fashioned — he used a proper fountain pen and all." He looked at Alice, no longer defiant. "D'you really think they could help?"

From his description these letters were written by the same person as the one in the case file. "It's possible," Alice said. "Our forensic people can get a lot from paper and possibly even the ink."

"Well, in that case . . ." he said. "Ellie wanted to burn the lot but I persuaded her to put some by. I thought they might come in useful one day — if we got hold of whoever wrote them like."

"Did you have any idea who might have written them?"

Laser shook his head. "I meet all sorts of weirdos in my line. Could have been anyone."

"Do you still have the letters?" Alice asked.

"Yeah, they're at my place somewhere. I know I didn't bin them."

"If I get an officer to give you a lift home, would you object if he helped you look?"

He folded his arms again. "What's in it for me? You know the way it goes. I help you so you need to do something for me."

Alice rolled her eyes. "What did you have in mind?"

"Whatever you think I've done, you forget about it. I help you and I'm as free as a bird."

That was fine with Alice. They'd only brought Laser in to ask him about Ellie in any case. There would be other occasions to nab him for the drugs. He wasn't the type to stay out of trouble for long.

"I'm dossing down with some mates in an empty house on the Langdale. If one of your lot is brave enough to take the risk and come there with me, you're on."

"We're not afraid of the Langdale, Laser. Anyone gets too ambitious and they'll find themselves behind bars," Alice said.

"Okay. But there's at least six of us in the house give or take, and stuff gets moved about. I've no idea where they might be."

"Not to worry. I'll leave you with Sergeant Hawkes here while I go and get it organised."

* * *

The letters, if they could be found, would be very useful. Alice was sure Jack Nevin would wring everything forensically

59

possible from them. Back in the main office, she sought out DC Neil Barrow. "A bit of excitement for you. I want you and DC Birch to take Laser back to his place and help him find some letters. He lives on the Langdale, hence the two of you." She saw the look; he wasn't keen. "Your job is to ensure that Laser doesn't do anything stupid, like destroy or hide the things. I want that letter, it could be an important piece of evidence."

Barrow shook his head. "Are we getting backup, ma'am? You know what that place is like. The rougher element get word that the coppers are looking for something and all hell could break loose."

"Don't worry, I'll have half a dozen uniformed officers in an unmarked van in the pub car park. Just find those letters and bring them to me."

CHAPTER THIRTEEN

The street was quiet, no sign of trouble. No doubt that would come later when the pubs turned out. Laser pointed to a mid-terrace town house daubed in graffiti.

"That's the one. The flat's on the ground floor."

"Will there be anyone else in there?" Barrow said hesitantly.

"You mean any of my crack-head mates," Laser laughed. "Don't worry. If there is they'll be sleeping it off. We made a night of it yesterday."

Barrow wasn't particularly comforted by this information. If Laser's friends had been taking drugs all night and were just coming round, they'd be in a bad state. He and Birch entered the house behind Laser. The place stank of beer and stale kebabs. Barrow flicked the light switch but nothing happened — no electricity.

He handed Birch a torch and made for what looked like a bundle of clothes on a battered old sofa.

"I'd leave him if I were you," Laser hissed. "Let him sleep it off. That one's got a right temper on him. Wake him and he's likely to blow up."

Barrow could see from the state of him that there was no chance of him coming round for a while, he was completely out of it. More worrying was the fact that he'd vomited, and on closer inspection, was barely breathing. Barrow looked up at Laser. "I think he's in a bad way."

"He'll be fine, just overdone it last night. He'll come round in his own good time. Just leave him."

But there was no way the young detective could do that. The lad was groaning in pain and struggling to breathe. "How old is he?"

"How should I know? Old enough — twenty something at least."

But Barrow was insistent. "Get searching for those letters," he told Laser and Birch. "I don't like the look of him. I'm going to ring for an ambulance. I won't be happy until he's had medical attention."

"And he won't be happy when he wakes up in hospital," Laser said.

"But he'll be alive," Barrow retorted. "I'm sure he'd prefer that."

"Where d'you reckon these letters might be?" Birch asked Laser.

"Try that set of shelves over there. Anything comes through the letterbox, that's where I stash it. But I have to warn you there was a stack of stuff here when we moved in."

Great, just what they needed. Birch got to work. "There are dozens of old bills — utilities and the like — in here. No one appears to have paid anything in months."

Laser grinned. "We don't do bills, hence no power."

Having put the lad in the recovery position, Barrow joined Birch. "Bloody hell. This could take hours."

"They were all in blue envelopes if that helps," Laser called out. "I remember because Ellie commented on it."

Nevertheless, it was a mammoth task. Barrow was tempted to shove the lot in bin liners and take it all back to the station where he could get others to help.

Suddenly there were flashing lights outside and a loud bang at the door. "The ambulance is here," Birch said, nudging him.

Two paramedics marched in. Barrow showed them his warrant card. "We're here doing a search and found him. I suspect he's overdosed. What on is anyone's guess."

Behind him, Laser sniggered. "It's not funny," Barrow said. "You know anything about the drugs he's taken then tell them."

"Looked to me like he took the lot," Laser admitted. "Crack, but mostly heroin. He'd had a row with his girlfriend and felt crap and this is how he's ended up."

"His name?" one of the paramedics asked.

Laser shrugged. "Freddie something. We tend not to ask. We get a lot of casuals staying here, doesn't do to get too involved with any of them."

"Okay, we'll take him to the infirmary on Oxford Road," the paramedic said.

Barrow began to search the lad's pockets. "Hang on, I've found a wallet. No cash but there is a bank card. His name is Freddie Whitton."

He put the wallet back and the paramedics made a note of the name. "Right, we'll be off."

While Barrow and Birch continued to search, Laser laid himself out on the sofa vacated by Freddie and closed his eyes.

"This is hopeless," Birch said after a while. "We could be here for days."

"You're right," Barrow said. "If we can find a couple of bin bags we'll take the lot away."

Birch went to look in the kitchen. "There's none in here, but there's a shop on the corner."

"Nah, I've a few carrier bags in the boot of my car, they'll do." Suddenly Barrow stopped. "Freddie Whitton. I know that name."

"From another case perhaps?" Birch said.

"No, it's connected to this case. That name is on the incident board back at the station. If I'm right, he's the lad who was going out with that missing Hewson girl."

"You sure? I mean if it is him what's he got to do with this little lot, and with Laser?" Birch said, keeping his voice low.

"It strikes me that a lot of aspects of this case lead back to that young man." Barrow looked over towards the sofa where Laser was now snoring his head off. "Carry on looking for the damn letters while I go outside and give our leader a call."

Whatever it might mean, finding Freddie Whitton dossing down with Laser couldn't be good. If Freddie was mixed up with the fledgling dealer in some way, the missing girl Maggie could be too.

Soon, Barrow was back in the house. "We're to leave Laser for now. He's not much good anyway, the state he's in. She also says we can bag this lot up and take it with us."

He got to work sweeping up the papers and shoving them into bags when something fell to the floor — a mobile phone. Glancing quickly back at Laser, who was fast asleep, he bent and picked it up. The phone was small, pink and covered in stickers, a girl's phone. He tried to turn the thing on but the battery was flat. It'd have to wait until they got it back to the station. If Ellie had stayed here, it may well have been hers.

CHAPTER FOURTEEN

Andrew Hewson had been brought to the station to make the appeal for help in finding his daughter. While the camera team got everything set up, Alice remained in the incident room weighing up the new information Barrow had brought back from the Langdale.

"Maggie's boyfriend, Freddie Whitton, is known to Laser, a person of interest in the murder of Ellie Fleming." She studied the board. "How come these young people all know each other, Hawkes?"

"Perhaps that's just it, ma'am, they're all young and they hang out in the same places."

"You mean pubs, clubs and the like. Maggie is a bit young for all that, surely?" she said.

Hawkes shrugged. "I'm not the one to ask. But these young girls can make themselves up to look a lot older than they really are."

But Maggie didn't live on the Langdale. Her dad had a decent income and she lived in a good part of town. Would he allow her to go out drinking? But would he even know? "We need to find out a great deal more about Freddie Whitton — where he comes from, his background and who his friends are. Maggie's dad seems to think he's okay but given you found him hanging out with Laser, chances are he's probably wrong. And Maggie wouldn't be the first young woman to fall for a bad boy."

"He did say that Freddie had left home, had a job and a reasonable income. I've checked, and he's never been in trouble. He works in Reagan's fitness club, ma'am. After Reagan's name was mentioned I checked him out. The gym is legit and has been operational for a couple of years. Freddie has been there since it opened."

Alice heaved a sigh. "That could prove tricky, particularly if Maggie went to see him there and got herself mixed up with Reagan and his thugs. I think we're going to have to pay that gym a visit."

"D'you intend to tell Hewson what we know, ma'am?"

Alice saw no benefit from doing that yet. "We tell Hewson only what he needs to know. There's still a question mark over his part in this."

* * *

Andrew Hewson performed his part well. Looking straight at the camera, he made an impassioned plea for his daughter's safe return. Having addressed her captor, he assured Maggie that she wasn't in any trouble and that all he wanted was to have her home again.

When he'd said his piece, Alice informed the public of the numbers to ring and who to contact. She too assured Maggie that all she had to do was pick up the phone. There would be no comeback.

"Will it do any good?" Hewson asked, watching the camera crew pack up their equipment.

"It'll certainly do no harm," Alice said.

He sighed. "Let's hope that wherever she is, Maggie sees the appeal and comes to her senses."

"Have you spoken to her friend Gemma?" Alice asked.

"Yes, and her mother. They know the score. Gemma's mother will stand no nonsense. If Gemma does know where Maggie is, her mother will get it out of her."

"And the boyfriend, Freddie?"

Hewson shook his head. "Maggie only ever spoke about him, we never actually met. The most she did was show me a photo of him on her phone."

"He's older than your daughter, you say?" Alice said.

"A couple of years, that's all, according to her anyway."

Alice knew that to be a lie. Freddie Whitton was in his mid to late twenties. "You'd better go home in case Maggie comes back. I'll get an officer to take you and he'll stay with you for a while, see if anything happens on the back of the appeal."

"And if it doesn't work, what then?" Hewson asked.

"Let's not get ahead of ourselves. If Maggie saw that appeal, she'll be in touch, I'm sure."

Only slightly reassured, Hewson left to go home.

Back in the incident room, Alice went to Hawkes's desk. "Fancy a visit to the gym? I think a word with Max Reagan is needed."

Hastily, Hawkes put his mobile in his pocket, looking flushed.

"Tricky call?" Alice asked.

"Beth," he said. "She's had to leave Lizzie with her mother because I'm not at home."

"Well, we all know what the job is like," she said. "I know it's not easy, trying to balance work and kids, I've been there, but there's not a lot we can do."

"I know, ma'am, and I'm not complaining. I just find it hard explaining to the family about how the job is. Beth's a nurse and she's down for a run of nights. The deal is that I'll get home at a reasonable hour. I have tried to explain but—"

"Okay. We'll get the visit to Reagan over as soon as we can and then you can get off." She smiled at him. "And apologise to Beth and her mother for me. I bet they think I'm a right harridan, don't they?"

He shuffled his feet. "Not at all, ma'am."

He was lying. Never mind, couldn't be helped. Hawkes had a future in CID and she didn't want to see him fail because of domestic issues. Those very same issues had almost done for her when her own son Michael had been small.

CHAPTER FIFTEEN

Max Reagan's gym was in Failsworth, partway between the city and Oldham. The building was new, and as far as Alice could see, had all the latest equipment, as well as a pool.

A young woman with a too-bright smile approached the pair. "Can I help? Only if you're looking to join, we're full at the moment."

Alice showed the woman her badge. "A word with Mr Reagan, please."

The woman put her hands on her hips. "You lot just can't leave him alone, can you? He turns his life around, doesn't put a foot wrong in months but still you hound him."

"We're not here to hound anyone," Alice said. "A quick word, that's all we want."

"Everything okay, Tracy?"

The speaker striding towards them was tall and muscular with close-cropped fair hair. It was immediately apparent from his demeanour that this was the man in charge.

"Max Reagan?" Alice asked, showing him her warrant card. "We'd like a quick word about an employee of yours, Freddie Whitton."

Reagan rolled his eyes. "Freddie's an occasional employee at best. He's workshy, can't get up in the mornings. If the lad showed a bit more willingness, he might do well, but what can you do. What's the young fool done, anyway?"

"When did you last see him?" Alice said.

"Two days ago. He went home sick at the morning break. A skinful the night before, I reckon. He hasn't rung in since but I expect he'll surface again when he's ready."

"He's currently in hospital with what we believe is an overdose of heroin," Alice told him. "We found him during a search of a house on the Langdale. Just as well we did, the lad was in a bad way. D'you happen to know who his friends are on the estate?"

"You're talking about that waste of space Laser, aren't you? Yes, I know Laser. I know him and half a dozen just like him." Reagan shook his head. "I had hoped for more from Freddie. He's basically a good lad but easily led. Laser, on the other hand, is someone I wouldn't trust an inch, he's very good at manipulating people, is Laser."

"Did you ever meet Freddie's girlfriend, Maggie?" she asked.

"She came here to meet him from work once, a few weeks ago. She's much younger than Freddie, isn't she? I seem to remember she was wearing a school uniform. She wasn't here long, Freddie finished what he was doing and the pair went off."

"Her full name is Maggie Hewson and she's missing. If by any chance she turns up here looking for Freddie again, ring me at once." Alice handed him her card.

"Kids. Enough to drive you mad." He tutted. "Anything else?"

"No, thank you, Mr Reagan, that's all for now."

She and Hawkes returned to the car. Alice couldn't make up her mind about Reagan. He didn't come across as a gangster, not even a reformed one. Was the bright shiny gym just a front? Whatever, the man had a past. Who's to say he wasn't still playing his old game.

* * *

"What d'you think?" Hawkes asked as she started the engine.

"He seemed honest enough to me, at least on the surface. Who knows? Perhaps he has turned his life around, but men like Reagan can't just give up being top dog after they've had a taste of power."

"Where to now, ma'am?"

"We'll go back to the station and you can get off home. I'll pay a swift visit to Freddie on my way home."

"I can come with you. Beth will have sorted Lizzie by now, so there's no rush."

"It's a tricky business, childcare. Best you get home and smooth things over. Give Beth my apologies when she comes off her shift."

"You're not to blame, ma'am. Like you said, it's the job."

Alice wished there was more she could do to help. Her sergeant's situation took her right back to the days when she'd been raising her son, Michael. Paul had been useless and childcare had been a persistent problem. In the end it had been Dilys who'd saved the day. Michael had spent most of his pre-school days with either Dilys or her sister, Doris. Something Alice would always be grateful for.

Alice dropped Hawkes off at the station and made her way to the hospital, half a mile up the road. Freddie Whitton had slept off most of the effects of whatever he'd taken and, apart from a thick head, said he was feeling more like himself.

"Your girlfriend, Maggie Hewson. She's missing," Alice said. "D'you have any idea where she could be?"

Freddie shook his head. "We had a row, that's mostly why I took the drugs. Stupid, I know, but she said a lot of hurtful things. After the row she stormed off. I presumed she'd gone home. I rang her loads of times but she wouldn't pick up."

"She also had a row with her dad. Did she tell you about that?"

"Yeah, and that was the problem. I told her to ring him and apologise. The guy has a tough time of it. He works hard, keeps house and sees to Maggie and she's not easy to deal with, believe me."

"She didn't apologise, Freddie. In fact, her dad hasn't heard from her since yesterday morning."

The young man looked genuinely worried.

"Does Maggie have any friends that her dad doesn't know about?" Alice asked.

Freddie shook his head. "She's closest to Gemma, they're at school together. Thick as thieves they are. But her dad knows her and her family."

"We've spoken to her, along with all of Maggie's other friends but none of them know anything about where she might be. You were my last resort, Freddie."

Freddie took his mobile from under the pillow and checked it. "I do have a load of missed calls from her. I'll have been out of it, not even able to answer. I'm sorry I can't be more help. I really like Maggie but she can be headstrong and this is a prime example. If she's gone off grid it'll be to punish her dad — me too possibly. We can only hope she surfaces soon."

So did she. "We found you in a house on the Langdale estate where Liam Lazelle — Laser — is currently living. How well d'you know him?"

Freddie looked away. "Everyone knows Laser. He's the dealer I generally get my stuff from. There are worse on that estate."

CHAPTER SIXTEEN

When Alice got home the house was in darkness. Dilys had left a note explaining that she hadn't had time to shop because her sister was ill and she'd had to go and look after her.

Alice opened the fridge and found a pack of ham not yet past its sell-by date. She was too exhausted to cook, a sandwich was about all she could manage.

Half an hour later, showered and in her dressing gown, she sat down with the sandwich and a mug of coffee and opened the case file. She was trying to decide if Maggie Hewson's disappearance was a separate case. If so, she should hand it over to another team and concentrate on the Ravenswood murders. But if it wasn't, what then?

An hour later, after a painstaking re-read of the paperwork, Alice came to the conclusion that there were just too many coincidences. Maggie's dad knowing Kendrick's. The Kendrick's factory overlooking the burial site. The bedsheets made by Kendrick's. Somewhere along the line the fact that Maggie was missing had to be connected. But how?

The trill of her mobile interrupted her thoughts.

"Maggie Hewson's mobile data has come in, ma'am," DC Barrow told her. "I would have left it for the morning but some of what was on there may be important."

"Go on."

"She made a number of calls during the day she went missing, and until four in the afternoon they all pinged the mast closest to her home."

Meaning that once her dad was out of the way, Maggie must have calmed down and stayed in.

"But then she got a call from an unknown number. They spoke for almost five minutes and the next time we pick her up is in Failsworth, where she rang Freddie's number but got no reply."

Alice was instantly on the alert. She had a pretty good idea where the girl was going. "Have you tried ringing the unknown number?"

"Yes, ma'am, it's Max Reagan's gym."

What was Reagan doing ringing a schoolgirl, Alice wondered. And why hadn't he mentioned the call when they'd spoken to him earlier?

Alice checked the time, not yet eight. The gym would still be open. "Meet me in the gym car park in twenty minutes," she said.

"Are you sure, ma'am? Don't you want to wait for DS Hawkes in the morning?"

"No, I want to get this done now."

Alice finished the call and went upstairs to get dressed. Ten minutes later, car keys in hand, she was on her way out.

* * *

Barrow was sitting in his car outside the gym. Alice tapped on his window and beckoned, and he followed her inside. At the reception desk, Alice held up her warrant card and barked, "Mr Reagan." She was in no mood for more of his lies.

Reagan appeared in a track suit, rubbing his head with a towel. "What is the meaning of this, police harassment? I've already told you everything I know."

"On the day Maggie Hewson disappeared, you rang her mobile and spoke for several minutes. After that, she must have come here, because her phone pinged a mast only metres away from this gym."

He held up his hands. "All right, I admit it. I did speak to the girl. I had loads of missed calls from her, so called her back. She came here in bits over Freddie and I was trying to calm her down. She kept going on about how she couldn't find him. I mean how was I supposed to know where the kid had gone?"

"That took over fifteen minutes, did it?"

"Like I said, the girl was upset. I took her into the office and got Tracy to make her a cup of tea. Turns out Maggie hadn't eaten all day so I sent out for a pizza. Once she'd calmed down, she agreed with me that the best thing to do was go home."

"A shame she didn't take your advice. Do you have any idea where else she might have gone?"

Reagan shook his head. "Look, I'm not an expert on teenage girls. I tried my best to help, but it's obvious from what you're telling me that she took no notice."

"This was Tuesday. What time?" Alice asked.

"About seven in the evening," he said.

"When she left here, did you see which way she went?"

"Yes, she hung about outside for a while so I offered to order and pay for a taxi but she was having none of it."

"Then what happened?" she asked.

"By then I was getting worried. There was no reasoning with the girl. I tried ringing Freddie's mobile but got no answer. I kept offering to see her home but she just got angry and stormed off. There was nothing I could do."

"And you just watched her walk away? A sixteen-year-old girl, upset and on her own."

"Don't you kid yourself, Inspector. That girl can hold her own in any confrontation. When I told her I'd no idea where Freddie was, she didn't believe me. Came at me with fists flying. I'm telling you, she has the temper of a she-devil."

This was getting her nowhere. "So, when Maggie *finally* left, which way did she go?"

"Towards the bus stop down the road from here. All the buses go straight into the city. She let a few go by and then got on one heading for Piccadilly."

Useful, and it made Alice wonder why Maggie would make such a trip. Did she have some idea of where Freddie might be?

"What do you think, ma'am?" Barrow asked when they were both back at the cars.

Alice checked her watch, it was late. "Tomorrow, you get on to the bus company and have a look at any CCTV they might have. She left the gym and got on a bus into town. I want to know where she got off and with luck, we may be able to track her from there."

CHAPTER SEVENTEEN

Thursday

The following morning Alice got a call from Hawkes to say that the letters sent to Ellie had been found.

"They don't make pleasant reading, ma'am. The writer lays into her for the life she's led but doesn't say exactly what he's accusing her of. He writes that she should think about her past, the people she knew, what she saw and did. He ends by saying she should be prepared to pay the ultimate price for her misdeeds."

Alice had no idea what that might mean. "She certainly paid for something. The problem is we know precious little about Ellie or her past. We can't even take a stab at guessing what the letters are referring to. What did she see and who did she know? Right now, we're clueless. Doesn't the writer give any hints at all?"

"No, ma'am. It's weird, the language he uses is strange, old-fashioned, and the spidery handwriting makes you think the letters were written way back in the past — you know, sort of ghostly. The style of writing, the paper and ink, are identical to the ones we received at the station. All except one, that is. The last one looks as if it was written by someone else."

Did this mean that the killer had known Ellie personally? From what Hawkes said it sounded that way. "Anything else?" she asked.

"The mobile that Barrow found is with Comms. They'll let us know the minute they have something."

"I want a full call list — to and from, and a printout of all the texts," she said.

"They'll be as quick as they can," he said.

"I'm on my way in," she told him. "Neil Barrow should be going through the CCTV from the bus stops between Failsworth and the city. Make sure there are enough eyes on that. We're looking for Maggie Hewson. She did go back to Reagan's gym. I put him on the spot last night and he admitted it. According to him she left in a mood and caught a bus into town."

"With respect, ma'am, chasing after Maggie is taking the team away from the main case."

He was right but what could she do. They had limited resources and couldn't just ignore a missing teenage girl. Furthermore, Alice couldn't be sure her disappearance wasn't connected to the murders. "Two hours tops this morning and then they can carry on searching those cottages near Ravenswood."

Was that a waste of time too? They were close to Kendrick's factory and she couldn't rid herself of the suspicion that someone who worked there could be involved. Spidery writing in old-fashioned black ink — those words were stuck in her head. She could think of only one person who might produce a document like that — Ralph Kendrick. He and his office were like something from a different age. Apart from the ancient ledgers, she had spotted bottles of ink and fountain pens on his desk. Alice decided she'd go along with the team and while they carried out the search, she'd have another word with Kendrick.

* * *

"Got anything?" Alice asked Neil Barrow as she went to put her jacket in the office.

"I've just spotted this, ma'am," he said. "Maggie got off the bus in Piccadilly and went into the café by the stop. The film isn't too clear but she talks to the man behind the counter for a minute or two and then he lets her through into the back."

Keen to join the cottage search party, she told Hawkes to go to the cafe. "One for you, I think. Find out what Maggie was doing there and where she went afterwards. Take Roger with you. Team briefing and feedback at four this afternoon."

"Freddie Whitton was released from hospital this morning," DC Tony Birch told her.

"We will no doubt need to speak to him again. I hope we have a proper address for him."

"All documented, ma'am," Birch said. "In fact, the young man appeared genuinely concerned that Maggie is still missing. Says he wants to help search for her."

"We'll let him know. Meanwhile, we'll see what Hawkes turns up from that café owner."

Alice looked at the incident board. There were more names there now, but also more questions. With a sigh, she took a look at her mobile. She had a missed call from Dilys, which was unusual.

Telling Barrow to wait a minute, Alice went into her office and rang Dilys back. The voice on the other end of the line was distraught.

"It's my sister," Dilys sobbed. "She died in the night. I don't know what to do. It's come as such a shock, I'd no idea she was that poorly. The doctor said she had a bad heart. She's been taking medication for years and never said anything."

Alice knew that the two sisters had been close and relied on each other. It must have come as a real blow. "I am sorry, Dilys, love. Is there anything I can do?"

"I'll need time off. There's only me, so I'll have to make all the arrangements. Will you manage all on your own in that big house?"

Typical Dilys. "Never mind me, I'm busy at the moment with work. More to the point, will *you* manage? Are you sure you don't need my help?"

"The neighbour will help out if needed. She's been friends with Doris since they were girls. I just need a day or two to get used to the idea of her not being here, then I'll be fine."

"Take as long as you need and don't go worrying about me, Dilys."

"You will eat, won't you? You won't go starving yourself now, or eating rubbish."

Alice smiled. Good old Dilys. "I'll be good, I promise."

CHAPTER EIGHTEEN

Alice stood and watched the group of uniformed officers make their way up the hill towards the cottages where a representative from the water board was waiting to meet them.

She and Neil Barrow continued towards the factory. Mrs Hubble opened the door, greeted them with a curt nod and led the way to Ralph Kendrick's office.

"He's not well, so don't upset him," she warned. "Your last visit did him no good at all. He's hardly eaten or slept ever since."

Alice gave her a tight smile. "That sounds to me like someone with a guilty conscience."

Mrs Hubble drew herself up to her full height. "All I can say is you obviously don't know him. The idea that you could think for one moment that he had anything to do with the murder of those girls shocked him to the core."

"We found it pretty shocking ourselves," Alice said. "But today we're here about something else." As they made their way through the factory workshops, she said to Barrow, "Stay here and have a word with the workforce. And make sure everyone gets a look at that photo of Maggie Hewson. You never know, she might have come here looking for her dad. And ask them about the sheets that don't make it to the shops — if anyone takes them for their own use, or Kendrick has arrangements with another firm and sells them on."

Mrs Hubble showed Alice into Kendrick's office. As soon as he laid eyes on her, the old man groaned.

"Not you again. What do you think I've done this time?"

"Tell me about Andrew Hewson," Alice began.

He flushed with anger. "Oh, Hewson. If you ask me, he's a difficult man to like, particularly after what he's done to my firm. He works for Smallshaws, the soft furnishings chain that's withdrawing their business. He appears to be touring the North of England telling suppliers that they're finished."

Having said his piece, Ralph Kendrick sat back in his chair, which seemed to swallow him. He suddenly seemed very tired, the lines on his face deeper. He looked very fragile, thin with long bony hands, for all the world like a man from another age. The sight of this shrunken figure gave Alice the creeps.

"It was our turn on Tuesday," he continued after a pause. "Came straight out with it, he did, just like that. Told me our working practices were outdated and that they would not be placing any more orders with us."

"That annoyed you, did it?" Alice said.

Kendrick fixed her with his gaze. "Very much so. It means the end for us and everyone who works here."

Ignoring his complaint, Alice asked, "Have you ever met Hewson's daughter, Maggie?"

"No, I haven't. I know nothing about his family circumstances. Why d'you ask?"

"She's disappeared," Alice said simply.

"Ah, I see what this is. Hewson gives us the push, his daughter goes missing, so you think the two must be connected."

"Not necessarily. I was merely asking if you'd ever met her."

"As I said, no."

"Maggie Hewson isn't the only young girl who's gone missing," Alice said. "As I said at our last meeting, we have recovered four bodies from the woods just below your premises. Our investigation has revealed that the last victim was the recipient of threatening letters from her killer."

Alice handed him a copy of the most recent letter. "Do you recognise this, Mr Kendrick?"

Kendrick took it from her and ran his watery eyes over the contents. "You think the style of writing is old-fashioned, therefore it has to have been produced by me. Well, you're wrong." He shook the page at her. "Have you thought that perhaps that's what the killer wants you to think? He's pointing the finger at me to divert suspicion from himself." He threw the page down.

Alice hadn't thought this. It took her aback. "Okay, who d'you know who'd want to do that?"

"No one I know of." He looked at her, almost smiling. "I'm not usually so angry. It's just that man Hewson and what he's done to us."

That might be true but catching sight of that letter had angered him. "I'd like to take some samples of your writing materials if I may. A pen, some ink and a couple of sheets of paper."

He glared at Alice and for a moment seemed about to refuse. Then he shrugged. "Take the lot if you want, but it won't do you any good. I have better things to do with my time than write people threatening letters."

* * *

Out on the factory floor, Neil Barrow was speaking to one of the workers, a machinist called Mary. "Missing girl?" she said. "What? Did she work here?"

Barrow shook his head. "No, too young. This one is still at school." He passed her the photo. "She's the daughter of the rep from Smallshaws, Andrew Hewson. You know him, I expect."

"He comes here but he don't bother with us," Mary said. "Mr Ralph always deals with him." She took the photo and studied it for a moment or two. "There's been no one like that round here, not that I can remember anyway."

Another machinist called Linda peered over their shoulders at the photo. "There was that row in here three weeks ago, remember, Mary? Between Mr Felix and that young girl. Oh yes, that's right — you'd gone off early to get your Terry from school. Well, the girl was wearing a school uniform and I'd never seen her before. Turned up late in the afternoon and nearly caused a riot, she did."

"Look closer," Barrow said. "Was this her?"

Linda squinted at it. "Yes, I think it was. Same uniform anyway. The thing I remember most is that hair, long and black. That day she came she had it up in a ponytail."

"Can you recall what the argument was about?" Barrow asked.

"She was going on about her boyfriend. She seemed to think he should have been given a job here in the firm, said he'd been cheated. She laid into Mr Felix something shocking. She said she knew all about him — Mr Felix that is. I remember that clearly. She made so much noise that Mr Ralph had to come out of his office. He was angry with the pair of them. He led Mr Felix away and told the girl to go home. As far as I'm aware, that's what she did."

"Did Mr Felix mention it at all later?" Barrow said. "You know, apologise to you all for the disturbance?"

"No. But Mr Ralph said it was just a misunderstanding and not to let it interfere with our work."

"This boyfriend," Barrow said, "did the girl mention his name?"

"No, but I got the impression he was one of the Kendrick family," Mary said. "But to be honest the girl wasn't making much sense."

Neil Barrow thanked the pair and went to find Alice, who was still in Ralph Kendrick's office.

"Got something?" Alice asked as she let him in.

"Maggie did come here." He looked at Kendrick. "She had a row with your brother, Felix. Apparently, you intervened." He handed him the photo. "D'you remember what the row was about?"

"That her, is it, the girl you're looking for? To be honest, I didn't take much notice of what she looked like. She wanted some information from Felix. I couldn't be bothered with the details. I told her to leave and instructed Felix to go home too. But whatever it was, knowing my brother it wouldn't be about anything that serious. He's far too frivolous and easily led."

"Maggie thought you should give her boyfriend a job here — does that jog your memory?" Barrow asked.

"No. Like I said, I didn't take much notice."

"We'll still need to speak with Felix," Alice said. "Where is he likely to be at this time of the day?"

Ralph Kendrick took a card from his desk and passed it to her. "He's at home — that's the address. He's not been well and hasn't been in to work much. His behaviour, Hewson's visit, it's all made his illness worse."

"We still have to interview him," Alice said. "He could have information that will help us find Maggie."

Ralph Kendrick sighed. "Do as you wish. Brother or not, there are times when Felix is a real liability."

CHAPTER NINETEEN

Hawkes found the café in a row of shops bordering Piccadilly bus station. The street outside was busy but the cafe was empty.

Hawkes asked the solitary man at the counter if he could speak to the manager.

"That's me. Carlo Moretti — manager, waiter, cook and general dogsbody."

Hawkes showed him a photo of Maggie. "D'you recognise this girl?"

Carlo Moretti took a quick glance and shook his head. "We get lots of young ladies in here, they come in for a coffee while they're waiting for a bus or tram. I can't possibly be expected to remember them all."

But Hawkes had noticed the way his face flushed, the immediate response. "Come on, Carlo. You can do better than that. This particular girl got off a bus, came in here and you showed her straight into the back, behind the counter."

"No one except the staff goes back there. We have to be very careful — health and safety and all that."

Hawkes shook his head. "Look, we have her on CCTV. It clearly shows this very girl early Tuesday evening, getting off a bus, walking through the door of your café and you showing her into a back room. If you like, you can accompany us to the station and we'll show you the footage."

This made Carlo nervous. His eyes darted around the café as if he were looking for a means of escape. "She was upset," he said after a few seconds. "I had to take her somewhere private to speak to her. Her name is Maggie and she does a few shifts here in the week. She was looking for someone, a girl called Gemma who also works here. She wanted to know if I'd seen her and when she was due in next."

"Did you tell her?"

Carlo shrugged. "Gemma doesn't work here anymore. I had to let her go. She wasn't right for the place."

"This is a coffee bar by a bus station," Hawkes said. "What sort of person are you looking for?"

"Someone who isn't into drugs and doesn't attract the dregs of this city to my door," Carlo retorted.

"You're saying this Gemma takes drugs? You know that for a fact, do you?" Hawkes said.

"She's an addict and she also does a bit of dealing on the side — her and that friend of hers are both into it."

They knew about Freddie but not that Maggie herself did drugs. That was new. "What was Gemma's response when you gave her the push?"

"Not good and nor was Maggie's when I told her. She marched in here and started demanding to see Gemma. I told her that neither she nor Gemma was welcome in here, and then I showed her the door."

"Her reaction?"

"She swore a lot, made threats. She said she had friends who'd beat me up and wreck my café if I didn't take them back. I only realised later what the pair had been up to. Maggie had been bringing drugs to work. There was this man who came in without stopping for a coffee or anything, she'd hand them over and he'd go straight out."

Hawkes raised an eyebrow. "And you had no idea?"

Carlo shook his head. "Stupid of me, I know. I should have seen that the people they attracted were the wrong sort of customer."

"We're talking about young teenage girls here," Hawkes said. "You make them sound like monsters."

"Believe me they can both be pretty scary. One of their friends who came in is a known dealer. I had to get rid of them. I don't want my café getting a reputation. This friend of theirs is a mess — too fond of the drugs and doesn't care what he has to do to get them."

"Who are you talking about?"

"Laser. And before you ask, I don't have a clue where he lives. He sometimes hangs around outside begging for money. He seems to be homeless, so occasionally I give him coffee and a sandwich but that's as far as it goes."

"Did Gemma or Maggie ever talk about a lad called Freddie Whitton?" Hawkes asked.

"Oh yes. He's Maggie's boyfriend and he's involved with Laser too. All I want is to be left alone to run my business. That was never going to happen with either of those girls behind the counter."

"What did you say to Maggie that time she came here?" Hawkes asked.

"I said that her friend wasn't here, and to go home and not come back, I couldn't help her."

"And she accepted that?"

Carlo shrugged. "Eventually, but she wasn't happy about it."

Freddie and Laser knew each other, so it was reasonable to assume that Maggie knew both of them too. Was it Laser who'd supplied the drugs they sold from the café?

"Look," Carlo said anxiously. "I don't want to get involved. Laser is dangerous. He's unpredictable and not afraid of using a blade. He's also got backup to call on. I talk to you lot and next thing you know, they'll be fishing me out of the canal. You can offer me all the protection you like but you won't be able to prevent it."

Hawkes could see that Carlo was genuinely afraid. Whatever Maggie Hewson had got herself mixed up in was dangerous, and the sooner they found her the better. He handed Carlo his card. "She comes back, you let me know straight away."

Hawkes and Wallis were at the door when Carlo said, "I can tell you one thing, Laser and Freddie both work for someone else, someone far more dangerous."

Hawkes turned back. "Any idea who?"

"No, just that he's new around here. Some sort of businessman, I heard. He's got Laser in his pocket and Freddie does what Laser tells him."

Hawkes raised an eyebrow. "And you?"

Carlo raised his hands. "I want no part of it."

Outside on the street, Hawkes asked Roger Wallis if he thought Carlo had been straight with them.

"He hasn't got the balls to lie to us," Wallis said. "An angry Laser would make mincemeat out of that bloke. Perhaps we should keep an eye out."

"I'll tell the boss, see what she has to say."

CHAPTER TWENTY

The Kendrick home was a huge stone pile in the hills above the Saddleworth village of Diggle. It was reached by a winding single track that badly needed maintenance.

"Living up here can't be much cop in the snow, can it, ma'am," said Neil Barrow as the car bounced over the rough ground. "You could be stranded for weeks."

"Beautiful old house though," Alice said as they drew closer. "Must have cost a mint, and the upkeep must be astronomical."

The suspension groaning, they turned into the drive and parked up outside the front door.

"How do we play this?" Barrow asked.

"I don't quite know what to make of the two Kendrick brothers," Alice said. "We ask questions but keep it civil for now. I want to know a lot more about them, particularly why Maggie Hewson went for Felix like she did."

They didn't have long to wait before a woman answered their knock.

Alice flashed her warrant card. "We'd like a word with Felix Kendrick."

The woman's face gave nothing away. She simply opened the door for them to enter and led the way down a wide hallway. "Mr Felix hasn't been well lately. He's prone to bouts of illness and depression. He sometimes spends days locked in his room refusing to speak to anyone, but I'll try for you." She showed the detectives into a large sitting room that looked out over the sloping lawns of the garden. "Can I tell him what this is about?"

Alice smiled. "We just want a chat, nothing too heavy."

With a shrug, the woman disappeared.

"What d'you think?" Barrow whispered.

"I think we need to have that word whether Mr Felix is in the mood or not," Alice said.

Barrow wandered over to the French doors. "That's one big garden."

"Fortunately, we have plenty of help." They both turned to see a man standing in the doorway. "I'm Felix Kendrick. I believe you wanted to speak to me."

From the notes on the board, Alice knew him to be five years younger than his brother. He didn't look it. Both men were old before their time. Felix had Ralph's white hair and his face had a sallow, haggard look about it. Indeed, he didn't look well.

"I'm told you had an argument with a young woman in your workshop a few weeks ago," Alice said. "Her name was Maggie Hewson, and I'd like to know what was behind it." Alice passed him Maggie's photo.

He took the photo. "I remember her. Feisty little thing she was. Came storming in and accused me of all sorts. I had no idea who she was or who she was talking about either. I put the entire incident down to a case of mistaken identity. I discussed it with my brother and we decided not to press charges."

"You considered calling the police?" Barrow was surprised. "Cause that much of a disturbance, did she?"

"I think she'd been drinking, either that or she was high on something. Anyway, we managed to see her off the premises and she never came back." He looked from one detective to other. "Why, what is she saying? I can tell you now, whatever it is, it didn't happen. She arrived, she said her piece and then she flounced off."

"Mistaken identity you say," Barrow said. "We've been told she was after a job for her boyfriend. It seems she thought the Kendrick family owed him something."

"Ah, I remember now. She was looking for a lad called Freddie. I've no idea who he is and I told her so."

"Mr Kendrick, we're here because Maggie is missing," Alice explained. "Given that she had some sort of beef with you, and that her father does business with your company, we'll be questioning the staff at Kendrick's further about the events of that day."

"Did do business with our company," Felix said. "According to my brother, Hewson has now dropped us."

"Have you had any contact with her since?" Alice asked.

"No. Why would I? She's a schoolgirl, certainly not old enough to be considered for a job with us."

Fair enough. Felix Kendrick was being straight with them. The answers he gave rang true and there was no reason he should know Maggie or why she'd be so angry with him and his brother. "That'll be all for now," Alice said, handing him a card. "If Maggie does get in touch, be sure to contact us. We are extremely concerned for her safety."

"She appeared to be the sort of young woman who could look after herself," he said. "Not someone I'd like to meet on a dark night, that's for sure."

Those were Max Reagan's words too, Alice recalled.

Felix Kendrick stepped out into the garden, while Alice and Neil Barrow made their way back down the hallway in the housekeeper's wake.

"I hope you haven't set him back," she said. "He's in a delicate state at the moment and can do without any added stress."

Alice gave her a smile. "A few questions won't hurt him, surely."

Mrs Latimer sniffed. "If you need to know anything else, there are other family members you can speak to."

Alice gave her a sideways look. "You said members plural. I thought Mr Felix Kendrick just had the one brother, Ralph."

"There's Miss Fiona — if you can find her — and she has a son."

"Fiona? You said 'if you can find her'. So where is she?" Alice asked.

"It's not my place to tell tales, I've said enough already. After all, the family are my employers and I owe them some respect. Besides, all I know about that time comes from gossip and things I've overheard."

By now they had reached the front door. Mrs Latimer stood holding it open for them with a look on her face that told them they'd get nothing more from her.

Back in the car, Alice rang the incident room, and asked for Hawkes, who was back from Carlo's café. She told him to check the records for the Kendricks' sister and her son. "I want names, addresses and a little background on them both. Did you get anything useful from the cafe?"

"Yes, ma'am. Apparently, Maggie and her mate Gemma were dealing from there. Both of them know Laser too."

"Not what Andrew Hewson will want to hear. Did the search party in the woods find anything?"

"No, ma'am. Those cottages have stood empty for years. As for the ones that are habited, we found nothing there either."

At least she could rule them out for now. "We'll be back shortly. Gather the team together and we'll brief them on what we've got."

CHAPTER TWENTY-ONE

Alice told the team what she'd learned about the Kendrick family. "There's a sister and her son out there somewhere, both of whom are persons of interest. Hence, I want them both found."

"But if they don't live local then they can't be involved, can they?" Roger Wallis said.

Alice finished the note she was making on the board and tapped it with her marker pen. "For starters, neither of the two brothers have mentioned a sister and I'm curious to know why. Also, I have a hunch. Maggie went to the factory and argued with Felix about her boyfriend, Freddie." She looked round at the team. "Think about it. Why would she do that? Why go there in particular? The machinists said Maggie was ranting on about Freddie being entitled to a job there. It's my guess that he too is a member of that family and she didn't like the way he was being treated. I want Freddie bringing in again. I also want some family background — quickly. This could be important."

While she spoke, Hawkes had been intent on his computer screen. "You're right, ma'am," he announced. "Fiona Kendrick — ten years younger than Felix, married to one Albert Whitton and they have a son, Freddie Whitton."

There were gasps around the room as the news sank in. That same Freddie Whitton who was involved with Laser and, what's more, was going out with Maggie. No way could there be two Freddie Whittons. "I wonder why neither of the brothers mentioned him," Alice asked. "They had no ostensible reason not to, and Felix had the perfect opportunity. I wonder what they're hiding."

"Freddie we know about. We can pick him up easily enough, but Fiona was reported missing," Hawkes said.

"Dig that report out," Alice said. "I want to know her last known movements. Where is Freddie staying?"

"He's still at that flat where we found him that time we went there with Laser," Barrow said.

"Just in case he gets wise to what we've discovered and considers doing a runner, get round there and bring him in. We need a word about that family of his. When was that report on Fiona filed?"

"Two years ago," Hawkes said. "She was last seen by the housekeeper leaving the family home carrying a suitcase. No one has set eyes on her since."

"This husband of hers, Albert, do we have anything on him?" Alice asked.

"Not much. It says here that he works as a self-employed gardener. He lives in a cottage somewhere Hollingworth way which he bought off the Kendrick family," Hawkes said.

"DC Wallis, ring Ralph Kendrick and get this Albert's address. Do we have anything back from Forensics? Anything on the letters sent to Ellie or the mobile found in Laser's flat?"

"Forensics are comparing the paper and the ink used for those letters with what we took from Ralph Kendrick's office. So far, we've heard nothing. Comms have unlocked the phone and once it's charged, they'll analyse the data."

Alice nodded. They were no closer to finding who killed Ellie and the other girls who were buried in Ravenswood but they had a deal more information now than when Leo Monk was running the investigation. The connection with Kendrick's was a real breakthrough, and that was down to

Maggie Hewson's disappearance, as well as the Kendrick connection.

"DS Hawkes, tell us about Maggie Hewson's dealing," Alice said.

"She has a part-time job at Carlo's Café by Piccadilly station. Her and Gemma take it in turns to bring in the drugs and hand them over to a designated pick up later in their shift. Carlo, the manager, found out and sacked the pair of them."

"I bet Maggie's father doesn't know that little gem about his beloved daughter," Alice said. "Do we know who was supplying the girls?"

"No, ma'am, but according to Carlo, there's only one person running the drugs trade these days."

"You're thinking Reagan," she said. "I wonder if the girls crossed him, particularly Maggie. From everything we've heard, that young lady has a temper on her."

"She did leave his gym, caught the bus and went into town to Carlo's so it would have to be after that," Hawkes said.

"It is still possible. Reagan could have had her picked up. Take a look at the CCTV along that road. We'll also get a warrant and search his premises."

"We're specifically looking for the girl, ma'am?" Wallis asked.

"We're looking for Maggie and any hint that Reagan is involved in dealing."

While she'd been talking, Neil Barrow had been on the phone to Kendrick and now had an address for Albert Whitton. "He wasn't keen to tell me, ma'am. Apparently, the family doesn't speak to Whitton, haven't done for a while."

"That could have something to do with Fiona going missing," she said. "You and Wallis go and see Albert Whitton first thing in the morning. Get him talking, particularly about the Kendrick family. We want anything and everything, so get him to dish the dirt."

CHAPTER TWENTY-TWO

Though it was barely lunchtime, Andrew Hewson had finished work for the day. He planned to spend the afternoon visiting some of Maggie's haunts, and speaking to those of her friends who were willing to talk to him. On his way into the house he picked up his mail and put his briefcase on the hall table. He'd grab a sandwich, change into something other than his suit and make a start, he decided. About to mount the stairs, he heard a noise coming from Maggie's bedroom. Someone had sneezed.

He stood at the foot of the stairs and called out, "Hello! Who's there? If you're after robbing the place, there's not a lot to take."

"It's me, Dad."

"Maggie!"

Taking the stairs two at a time, he ran into her room. Maggie was just crawling out from under her bed, her kitten Molly in her arms.

"I got scared. I didn't know who it was. It's a bit early for you to be home," she said.

"Are you okay? Where the hell have you been? I've been worried sick. I've had the police out looking for you, told the papers, I've even been on the telly." His relief at seeing her was beginning to turn into the old anger.

"Yes I know. I'm sorry, Dad, but I had no choice. I started off looking for Freddie but then I got into a bit of bother and had to lie low."

A bit of bother? His stomach began to churn. "What sort of trouble, Maggie? Something to do with that boyfriend of yours?"

She hesitated, obviously wondering if she should tell him the truth.

"Look, love, this has gone on far too long. I can't help you if you won't tell me what's wrong." She gave him that look, the one he knew so well. There were any number of things she wasn't telling him.

"Has someone threatened you?" Hewson didn't know why he'd asked that but there was something in his daughter's eyes that he hadn't seen before, real fear. She nodded, on the verge of tears.

Hewson was livid. His hands curled into fists, and he had an overwhelming urge to knock someone's head off. "I get my hands on that Freddie Whitton and he'll never threaten anyone again."

"It wasn't him," she said. "No, this is down to someone else. A *proper* gangster is what Freddie told me, not someone playing games. He means it too, Dad. This man kills people."

"What the hell have you got yourself mixed up in, Maggie?"

Maggie was now crying in earnest. "Please don't get mad at me. I'm sorry I stropped off like that but I was angry. I intended to stay with Freddie for a couple of days but he'd gone walkabout and wasn't answering his mobile. I wanted to come home but I was scared that gangster would find me. I nearly rang you last night but then everything went wrong."

Hewson put his arms around her. "Want to tell me about it?"

"I can't. I tell you and you'll be in danger too. I'm not talking about some kid who's handy with his fists. This is a grown man, Dad, and he doesn't play around."

"The woman I'm dealing with is sympathetic and fair-minded. She'll help sort out your problems, and if you are in as much danger as you reckon, she'll put both you and Gemma somewhere safe until this is over."

"Witness protection," Maggie said with a grin. "How cool is that."

"This is no joke, Maggie. She will want to speak to the both of you. And she'll expect some cooperation."

"She'll want us to grass?" Maggie asked, shaking her head. "I don't know about that."

"You don't have a choice. We need their help but DI Rossi will want to know who you're so afraid of."

Maggie nodded. "Okay. I'll ring Gemma. If she agrees I'll get her to come round and we can get on with it."

"What I don't understand is how you got involved with someone so dangerous in the first place."

"He's Freddie's boss at the gym. When Freddie told him where I worked, he said he would give me and Gemma the chance to earn some easy money. All we had to do was follow instructions."

"Are you talking drugs, Maggie? Is that what this is all about?"

Maggie nodded. "I . . . think so."

"What sort of drugs, d'you know?"

"Either me or Gemma had to pick up a bag from a locker at the gym and take it to the café. I had a peek once and it was full of little packages — baggies as they're known on the streets."

"What do you do with the bag?" her dad asked.

"We pass it on."

"But someone must have noticed. What about your boss at the cafe? The police?" he asked.

"Carlo keeps his nose out of it. He's too scared, I reckon. As for the police, they don't bother us."

"Well, they will now," Hewson said. "Ring Gemma, get her to come here and I'll ring DCI Rossi."

CHAPTER TWENTY-THREE

Alice put the office phone back on the hook. "Hawkes you're with me. Maggie Hewson has turned up."

"Is she okay, ma'am?"

"She's at home with her father. He says she's fine physically but is very afraid. She got herself mixed up in drug dealing and is terrified some gangster will come after her. Anyway, her father has persuaded her to talk to us and tell us what she knows."

Hawkes shook his head. "And there was us thinking her disappearance was down to a spat with her dad."

"She is involved with Freddie Whitton don't forget, which means she has no doubt met Laser too. Her dad has every right to be concerned."

When they got to the Hewson home Gemma and her mother were already there. Maggie was huddled in a corner of the sofa playing with her phone.

"Are you girls both okay?" Alice asked. "We'll do this more formally at a later date but today all I want is for you to tell me where you've been and what's been happening to you."

Between them, the two girls related the entire sorry tale. When Maggie failed to mention something, Gemma filled in the detail. It didn't take long for Reagan's name to come up. Not that Maggie directly pointed the finger. Her face said it all, she was afraid. And knowing Reagan's reputation, with good reason.

"He is known to us," Alice told Hewson. "He comes across as a fine upstanding citizen. There is no denying that he's a successful businessman, a pillar of the community who provides employment for people in the area."

"Surely the girls' statements will enable you to nail him," Hewson said. "Especially if they identify him."

"The statements will help but we need to back them up with solid evidence. If we don't, his lawyers will argue that it's personal, and the girls have something against him, for example the way Reagan treated Maggie's boyfriend, Freddie."

"Is there anything you can think of, Maggie?" Hewson asked.

She and Gemma both shrugged. "I don't know what you mean by evidence," Maggie said.

"Okay, let's look at what else you can tell us," Hawkes said. "D'you know anything about where Reagan got the drugs?"

"Freddie told me that someone comes to the gym twice a week and does the drop."

Now they were getting somewhere.

"D'you know which days this happens?" Alice asked.

Maggie frowned. "He might have said but I wasn't really listening. It could be Friday though. I work on Friday afternoon and evening and there was always a bag ready to pass on."

"What did you have to do exactly?" Alice said.

"There's a bag left for me in a locker in the back room at the gym. I'm supposed to take it to work and hand it over when I've finished for the day. Someone meets me outside the café," Maggie said.

"D'you have a key for this locker, or does someone unlock it for you?" Hawkes asked.

"Not all of them have locks," Maggie said. "There is a notice on the wall telling people not to leave valuables in them."

Pity, thought Alice. Your average barrister would argue that in that case, anyone could have planted the drugs.

"Do you know the person who leaves the bag?" Hawkes asked.

"It's usually Sefton, a trainer who works for Reagan," Maggie said.

Alice checked her watch. She had ordered a search of Reagan's properties and she wanted to know if anything had been found yet.

She went out into the hallway to make the call. The team needed to get this right. It was their chance to nail Reagan, he'd got away with it for far too long. Roger Wallis answered.

"Got anything?" she asked him.

"Not yet, ma'am. The gym's pretty extensive."

"The girls have told me that before they're distributed, the drugs are kept in a room at the back. Get the dogs in, have them take a sniff around. The minute you get anything, ring me back straight away. If there is a man called Sefton hanging around, keep an eye on him. You find anything suspicious, bring him in."

"Reagan is kicking off, ma'am. Reckons this is police harassment and has rung his solicitor."

"He can complain all he wants. You have a warrant and when you do find something, he won't have a leg to stand on."

Alice went back to the girls. She had to tell them something positive so they'd put their trust in her. "We're searching the gym now. We find something and Reagan will be arrested. This Sefton too."

"What about the girl's safety?" Hewson asked. "This gangster won't hold back. He suffers because of what the girls have told you he's bound to want revenge, if only to demonstrate what happens to people who run to the police."

He was right, of course. Reagan wasn't likely to let this go. "Reagan won't know that it's you who've told us," she said. "After all, you're Freddie's girlfriend and you passed on the drugs. But just in case, we will keep you somewhere safe for a few days until Reagan is arrested."

As she spoke, her mobile trilled. She went back out to the hallway to take Wallis's call.

"The dogs have picked up something, ma'am. And we've found several bags of what looks like heroin stashed in a gym bag in a locker."

Brilliant! That was just what she wanted to hear. "Bring him in. I'll be back shortly."

Reagan had become sloppy, so confident that no one would dare grass on him that he hadn't even hidden the drugs properly. Alice was looking forward to banging him to rights.

CHAPTER TWENTY-FOUR

Max Reagan was brought to the station and put in a cell to await interview. His solicitor was arguing the toss with the desk sergeant when Alice arrived back.

"Problem?" she asked.

He gave her his card and introduced himself. "Dominic Stubbs. You're holding my client Mr Reagan and I'd like him released at once. I've tried telling this halfwit but he won't listen."

"We've arrested Mr Reagan on a drugs charge, so I'm afraid he won't be released any time soon," Alice said.

"I don't think you understand," Stubbs said. "You've got this all wrong. It won't be my client who's at fault but one of his staff or customers. He does his best for the community, he gives jobs to all and sundry in an effort to rehabilitate them but they just take advantage. There is very little in the way of security in his gym. Most of the lockers are left open. I have told him any number of times that this sort of thing could happen." He smiled at her. "Max wants to help everyone, you see, give them a chance to go straight, get clean, but obviously it doesn't always work."

This didn't sound like the Max Reagan Alice had met. "You're saying that what we found is down to someone else?"

"Precisely. No way would Max be so stupid. He employs a number of young people on a part-time basis. His customer base is also somewhat dubious in my opinion. Any one of them could be responsible for the drugs you found."

Alice didn't believe a word of it. "We'll see what he has to say for himself when we interview him. The drugs found on his premises isn't the only evidence we've got. I'll let you know when Mr Reagan is due to be interviewed."

Alice left the solicitor pacing up and down in the foyer and took the stairs up to the incident room. The solicitor was right. They needed evidence linking Reagan to the drugs or he would walk.

"This Sefton character, have we found him?" she asked the team.

"We've put the word out and got people looking, ma'am," Hawkes said. "The problem is that if he hears we're looking for him, he's likely to disappear into the underbelly of the city and we'll have no idea where to look for him."

"Let's hope not. I want him finding and bringing in. I want a statement. Sefton's evidence is needed if we're to put Reagan away."

"We found heroin on Reagan's premises, ma'am," Hawkes said, "a large quantity too, definitely not for personal use."

"Reagan's solicitor is bleating on about one of his staff or customers having put it there. According to him, Reagan practically runs a charity, doling out second chances and getting royally taken advantage of for his trouble. He spouts the same tale and we'll struggle to make the case stick."

"What about the girls?" Hawkes asked.

"They're sixteen and didn't actually deal with Reagan in person. Maggie says she handed the money over to Sefton. All Reagan offered her was a chance to make some extra money, which could mean anything including working in his gym. He could argue that as far as he was aware the gym bag contained nothing more dangerous than training shoes."

"In that case we need to find this Sefton quickly before we're obliged to release Reagan," Hawkes said.

"If we get Sefton to talk we'll have enough of a case to take to the CPS," Alice said.

Hawkes tossed his pen onto the desk. "He's going to walk, isn't he? We've got one of Manchester's biggest dealers locked up and we don't have enough to keep him."

Hawkes was right. As things stood, if they got Reagan to court, his expensive solicitor would get him off. "We've yet to speak to Freddie Whitton and Laser," she said. "Reagan has had dealings with both those young men. Perhaps they can be persuaded to give evidence?"

"I wouldn't bank on Laser telling us anything, ma'am. He's far too streetwise and will be aware of the consequences of double-crossing Reagan."

"Sefton, Laser and Freddie. Surely one of them will talk to us," Alice said. "We need to speak to Freddie anyway. DC Barrow, go and bring him in."

"All this is very well, ma'am," Hawkes said, "but it's distracting us from the main case. True, we've moved forward but we've still to find who killed those girls."

He was right. It wouldn't be long before Alice would have to decide whether or not to hand Reagan over to the drug squad and let them find the necessary evidence.

Alice went to her office to check for messages on her mobile. She was concerned about Dilys and how she was coping with the loss of her sister. But there was nothing. She was about to give her a call when the office phone rang. It was the desk sergeant downstairs. To her surprise, it wasn't Reagan's solicitor but a young woman.

"Says her name is Louise Morley, ma'am."

Alice recognised the name. Ellie's mother, Gloria, had mentioned her. "Did she ask for me by name?"

"Yes, ma'am, and she's insisting that you'll want to hear what she has to say."

CHAPTER TWENTY-FIVE

Alice had Louise taken to an interview room and she and Hawkes went to speak to her. Louise Morley was indeed young, no more than twenty. She was short with long fair hair and so thin that Alice feared that if she bent over, she might snap in two.

"It's about the girls you found in the woods," Louise said as soon as they walked in. "I knew them."

Alice guessed at once that Louise was the fifth girl. Ellie's mother, Gloria, had said there were five of them, and they had found four bodies. "Would you like to tell us about them," she said.

"We were all friends when we were young kids. For a while we went around in a group. Me and Ellie were still in contact, we rang each other regularly, but about two months ago she stopped calling. I tried ringing her any number of times but she never picked up."

Alice thought of the pink mobile found at Laser's flat. "I'm afraid Ellie has been murdered, your other friends have too," Alice said gently.

Louise turned pale. "I knew it. I sensed that something awful had happened to them."

At least Louise had cleared up one puzzle. These weren't random killings. "We believe that your friends were all murdered by the same man. We think he chose them because of something they knew or saw in the past. I wanted to talk to you in case you could shed some light on what that might be. There must be something you all had in common."

Louise looked down. "I always hoped I'd never have to talk about it."

"Talk about what, Louise?" Alice asked. "If you know something you have to tell us so we can catch this man."

"For a while we were all runners for a big-time dealer. My boyfriend got us into it. He said the job was a breeze and we'd make a packet. We were young and ignorant, in our early teens, dazzled by the thought of all the money we'd have to spend. None of us saw further than that. We never considered the implications of running drugs — the danger, the harm we might be doing."

"Does this dealer have a name?" Alice asked.

Louise shook her head. "I tell you that and I'm dead."

Alice knew she needed to tread warily if she was to get Louise to trust her. "What about this boyfriend of yours? Can you tell me about him?"

Louise shook her head. "I daren't."

"Okay. So, this man, this dealer, do you believe it was him killed your friends, or had them killed?"

"I don't know. He didn't like us much, I know that. He always thought we were on the rob — you know, creaming off our customers' money for ourselves. After a while someone new took over and things improved."

"This new person, the dealer who took over, want to tell me about him?"

"I daren't talk about him either. I still see him around and he knows me."

Reagan, Alice decided. "So, what did you think had happened to your friends?"

"At the time I didn't really concern myself about them. Then one day I woke up, realised what I'd got myself into and did one," she said.

"Why come back now?" Hawkes asked.

"I knew you were looking for me because I bumped into Ellie's mum soon after I got back home. She told me about the bodies and what had happened to Ellie."

Louise still had her gaze fixed on the floor. "It's hard talking about it. Ellie and I were close once. I've wracked my brain trying to work it out but all I can think of is that all four of them must have crossed the dealer in some way. He didn't give second chances, I know that much." She pulled a face. "I want to help but I can't. I tell you his name and he'll know it must have been me."

Time to backtrack a little. What was needed here was small steps if Alice was to tease a name out of her. "Was one of the four girls called Josie?"

"Yes, Josie Jones. She was the quiet one, wouldn't say boo to a goose. Her and Ellie were close at one time. The others were Katie Hammond and Sara Fletcher."

"You said you and the other girls went around together as a group," Hawkes said. "Even after you were older?"

"Sort of. We all came from the Langdale, knew the same people, went to the same school. We also knew all the dealers and who was the best one to score from. We were more or less the same age too."

"And you think this dealer is the only person who might want you dead?" he asked.

Louise nodded.

Alice was glued to the girl's every word, trying to match what she said with the reports on Reagan. The problem was, the way those girls had been killed simply wasn't his style.

"You can trust me, Louise. Really. If you tell me who he is, I promise we will keep you safe. We can take you somewhere he won't find you. Think about your friends, what would they want you to do?"

"We weren't perfect," Louise said slowly. "We got into trouble and not everyone liked us but they didn't deserve that."

Louise still wouldn't meet her gaze. She fiddled with a ring on her finger, crossed and recrossed her legs. Alice didn't have time for this, she needed the truth if she was to protect the girl.

"No, they didn't. They suffered too. They were kept somewhere, starved and beaten and made to stitch their own shrouds." Alice reached forward and put her hand on Louise's arm. "I want this man, Louise, both men. I want to put them behind bars where they belong, so they can't harm anyone else."

Louise wiped tears from her face. Alice had upset her. "Where are you staying?" she asked. "Given what you've told us we have to presume that you are now a target too. Whoever killed your friends will want to finish the job."

That rattled her. Louise stared at Alice with wide eyes. "I'm staying with my gran. I don't want anything to happen to her."

"On the Langdale?" Alice asked.

"No, she lives in Droylsden. Please, you have to protect us. If she gets hurt I don't know what I will do."

"We'll take your address and have an officer watch the house," Alice said. "Whoever killed your friends is serious, Louise. I strongly suspect that you are now high on his hit list. If he suspects for a moment that you're back in the area, he will come after you."

Alice didn't want to frighten the girl out of her wits but she had to make her understand the danger she was in.

"I didn't realise. I couldn't bear it if anything happened to Gran." Finally, her eyes met Alice's. "If I tell you, you will keep us safe, won't you?"

Alice crossed her fingers under the table. "Yes, we will." She gave her a moment and then said, "This dealer you're afraid of. Is it Max Reagan?"

Louise looked surprised. "Max? No, I doubt he'd harm us. The one I'm scared of is from the days before Max was king."

Alice wondered who that could be. No one she could recall had ever been that evil.

"We all worked as runners for him. He doled out the gear and we delivered it. We mostly worked in pairs. That's how me and Ellie got close. The money was good and there was very little hassle. But then I wised up. I realised that sooner or later we'd get caught. I didn't fancy going to prison so I legged it. I got as far away from the Langdale as I possibly could."

"You've done the right thing in coming to me," Alice said. "I just wish you'd trust me and give me a name. I'll get one of my officers to take you home."

* * *

"Louise and the other girls were working as runners for some unnamed drugs baron but she says it's not Reagan," Alice told the team.

"Not Reagan? That's a surprise. Is she lying? Afraid he'll go after her?" Barrow said. "Does that mean we are now considering this unnamed dealer for the Ravenswood murders. I must say if she'd said it was Reagan it'd have made our task a whole lot simpler."

"Of course she could be lying," Hawkes said. "But come on, we surely aren't considering Reagan as a suspect for the murder of those girls. It's just not his style. Think about how they were killed, the way they were dressed. A bullet through the brain is more Reagan's MO."

"Let's forget Reagan for the time being," Alice said. "We now have an unnamed suspect, someone we know nothing about."

Hawkes didn't look convinced. "Are you sure Louise is telling us the truth, ma'am? She's not trying to throw us off the scent with her tales of some villain we've never even heard of."

"Louise is scared and I've promised her protection." Alice turned to Barrow. "Get that organised for her, along

110

with the Hewsons, Gemma and her mum. I'll ask Forensics to check the bodies again and see if they can find anything that will lead us to Reagan or this unnamed person."

Hawkes shook his head.

"Unless we find something to the contrary, we are going with the theory that either Max Reagan or an unknown are our prime suspects for the killing of those four girls," Alice said. "What we concentrate on now is gathering the evidence to convict."

CHAPTER TWENTY-SIX

Friday

Neil Barrow and Roger Wallis were at the front door of Albert Whitton's cottage. "You mean someone actually lives in this dump?" Barrow said. "It's fit for nothing but tearing down."

Wallis could see what his colleague meant. The cottage sat in the middle of a large tract of land and had a spectacular view of the hills, but it had been left to go to rack and ruin. Nothing had been done to the house or the garden in what looked like years.

"He's a gardener too," Wallis commented, surveying the knee-high weeds. "You'd think at least he'd make an effort with that."

"Let's get this waste of time over with," Barrow said.

"We don't know that," Wallis said. "This man is connected to the Kendrick family and until we found out about Reagan, the boss was convinced that one of them was responsible for the deaths of those girls."

"She's not said as much," Barrow replied. "Anyway, let's face it, the boss is clueless and she's wasting her time hounding Reagan. We all know that what happened to those girls is not his style. Now this little detour. We need to get on with the job and stop pissing about."

"DCI Rossi is nothing if not thorough and she trusts her instincts," Wallis said, giving the dilapidated front door a bang. "I've worked with her before and take my word for it, her instincts are spot on." He pounded the door again, sending flakes of paint to the ground. "Mr Whitton! Are you there?"

"What d'you want?" The croaky voice came from behind them, his words followed by a prolonged bout of coughing. "You're trespassing, and I don't take kindly to folk wandering over my land."

The man who'd addressed them looked as unkempt as the cottage. He wore an old jumper that was fraying at the elbows.

"Albert Whitton?" Barrow asked.

"Who wants to know?"

"We're police," Wallis told him, flashing his badge.

"That means nowt to me. This is my land, and I want you off it."

"A quick look round, that's all we want. Surely you can't object to that."

Whitton coughed again, cleared his throat and spat. "Well, I have. I don't want strangers poking around my home, and particularly not the bloody police."

"When was the last time you saw your wife?" Wallis asked.

"Why, what's she done now?"

"Just answer the question, Mr Whitton," Barrow said.

"She walked out a couple of years ago and I haven't seen her since. Good riddance, that's what I say."

"D'you mind if we come in?" Wallis asked. "We'll have a quick look around and we'll be out of your hair."

"Yes, I bloody well do mind. This is my home, so do one or I'll set the dog on you."

This wasn't going to be easy. Barrow could see the day stretching out in front of him. They had better things to do than waste their time trying to reason with Whitton. "Okay, if that's how you want to play it, we'll leave you in peace, but you've not seen the last of us. We'll be back with a warrant and believe me you won't want that. It'll give us the right to tear the place apart if we see fit."

"Do what you want. There's nowt to find here, never was. You're wasting your time and mine."

"A foolish decision," Wallis told him. "An hour tops and this could be done and dusted."

Suddenly Whitton shouted, "*Wolf!*" Immediately they heard a dog barking inside the house, scratching at the door. Whitton gave the pair a little smile. "I open that door and he'll tear you to shreds. Now get off while you can."

Having little choice in the matter, the pair returned to the car.

"D'you reckon the man is hiding something?" Barrow asked.

"Difficult to tell," Wallis said. "Perhaps he's just being obnoxious. On the other hand, he could be hiding something."

"He's older than I imagined," Barrow said. "Freddie's only twenty odd but his dad looks ancient. He's frail too — and did you hear that cough? I doubt he'd be capable of overpowering teenage girls, even if they were half-starved."

"We'll only know for sure when we get that warrant and take a good look round," Wallis said. "Besides the house there's also a number of outbuildings down at the bottom of the garden. Given the location and how unpleasant Whitton is, anything could go on here and no one would know. We mustn't forget that Whitton does have a link to Reagan through Freddie. Look over there." Wallis pointed to a brand-new, top-of-the-range sit-on lawn mower. "Ask yourself, where did the money come from to buy that little beauty."

Barrow shrugged. "He must earn something from this tip he lives in. Perhaps he got the money selling scrap metal."

Wallis smiled at his colleague. "Or he could have given Reagan the use of one of those outbuildings. We'll speak to the boss and see what she thinks. If she still wants this place searching, she'll have to sanction a warrant anyway. Whitton wouldn't let us in for a reason. He's hiding something all right, you mark my words."

Barrow shrugged. "I just want that old bugger sorting."

CHAPTER TWENTY-SEVEN

Freddie Whitton was as good as his word. The uniformed officer who went to pick him up found the young man at Laser's flat just like he'd said.

Telling the officer he felt unwell, he nevertheless accompanied him back to the station. He seemed perfectly willing to help until Alice mentioned Reagan.

"I have nothing to say. Anyway, I'm supposed to be taking it easy. When I was in hospital with the overdose they discovered I was recovering from pneumonia, contracted when I spent a brief spell sleeping rough. That was down to me desperately trying to avoid Reagan's thugs. A misunderstanding about nothing and I have to run for my life. You have to understand my position. Reagan gets wind that it was me who grassed him up and I won't last the week."

"We can protect you," Alice said.

"No, you can't. What you don't realise is that Reagan has people on the inside, on his payroll, including some of your officers."

Alice didn't believe him for a minute. Granted, half the team were new to her but she'd had a good look at their personnel records and found no reason there to distrust them. "Look, Freddie, all I'm asking is for you to tell me about the procedures for transferring the drugs from Reagan's gym to the buyers. We already have statements from two others regarding distribution of the drugs but we need collaborative evidence from someone on the inside."

Alice watched him wrestle with this. He seemed to be on the brink of saying something when Hawkes appeared at the door and beckoned urgently to her. Annoyed, she followed him out into the corridor.

"Sefton was found dead this morning, ma'am," Hawkes told her. "His body was dumped in an alley in Ardwick. It was cleanly done — a single shot to the temple and no signs of a struggle."

"All the hallmarks of an assassination," Alice said. "Any witnesses, CCTV? Anything?"

"There are no cameras in the alley and no one saw anything either. I've got a team looking at CCTV from the surrounding area. You never know, we might get lucky."

So that was that. They could scrub Sefton as a witness, and Freddie would be too afraid to tell her anything now. Unless she could turn Sefton's murder to her advantage, but how? There was no point in keeping it under wraps. Freddie would learn the truth the moment he hit the streets.

She went back into the room. "Sefton has been shot through the head. His body was found dumped this morning." She paused, giving him a few moments for this to sink in. "We don't want the same thing happening to you, Freddie, so talk to me before it's too late."

"Sefton, dead!" He looked shocked. "See, it's just like I said. There's no way I can grass now — they'll just shoot me too."

Alice knew she wouldn't be able to convince him, not yet anyway. "I understand where you're coming from, but look — we get Reagan, put him away and you'll be free of the danger."

Freddie Whitton shook his head. "You must think I have a death wish. I can't tell you anything, so stop asking."

Time for a change of tack. "Weren't you ever curious about what happened to your mother, Freddie?"

His head shot up. He hadn't expected this. After a while, he said, "She left us, simple as that. I reckon she couldn't stand living with my father. She'd had enough of his penny-pinching, dictatorial ways. Frankly, I don't blame her. My only regret is that she didn't take me with her or at least tell me what she'd planned."

"Did you ever wonder why that was?"

"Yes, many times. In the end I decided she'd make contact later, maybe when she got settled."

"But she didn't. That must have hurt. Has she ever tried to get in touch with you?"

"No, not even a text."

"Poor you. You were hardly a child but even so, have you ever asked yourself why your mother acted like that? Mothers usually cannot bear to leave their children."

"If she had contacted me my father might have found out and gone after her. He blames her for most of the ills in his life. It's madness, of course, but I could never persuade him otherwise."

"D'you see much of him?" Alice asked.

"As little as possible. He's an obnoxious little man, full of his own importance, who doesn't give a stuff about anyone else. I gave up on him a while ago."

Alice could see from his face that Freddie meant every word. "That's an interesting cottage he lives in, so my detectives tell me."

"It's a dump. I once looked at the land registry records to check that he actually owned it. He used to rent it from the Kendricks until he bought it off them for a nominal sum. Pity he didn't sell up when the place was in a better condition. He might have got a bob or two then at least."

He'd been candid with her about his dad. It was just a shame he wouldn't talk about Reagan in the same way. "How did you get involved with a man like Max Reagan? I had an idea you'd set your career sights higher."

"My mum made him promise that if I ever needed a job, he was to employ me. After I gave up on uni I was penniless, so I went to see him. He was only too happy to help and took me on."

"Reagan knew your mother?" said Alice, surprised.

He smiled. "The pair were an item for a while. Proper loved up they were. She went everywhere with him. After she'd been seeing him for a while, she decided she'd had enough of my dad. Reagan must have encouraged her or she would never have dared. When she went missing and I learned she wasn't with Reagan, I was surprised. I couldn't think of anywhere else she'd go."

"Did you ever ask Reagan about her?" Alice said.

"She rang him the day she left the cottage. They were supposed to meet but she never turned up. That's what he told me, and I've no reason to disbelieve him. Believe it or not he was actually quite cut up about her no show."

The link between Fiona Whitton, nee Kendrick, and Max Reagan was ringing all sorts of bells in Alice's head. She needed to give serious thought to this new development.

"Ellie, who stayed at the flat with Laser, had three friends who were also murdered," she said. "We've been told that was down to Reagan. Apparently, all four, plus a fifth girl, worked as runners for him."

"He's not in the habit of killing his people, not unless they cross him in some way. But these were just young girls, you say?" Freddie shook his head. "How did they die?"

"Brutally. We think they were imprisoned for a while first, and they all had their hands cut off."

"Are you sure it is down to Reagan? That's just not his style. A bullet to the head and dump the body is how he operates. He doesn't go in for slow torture."

From what Alice knew of how Reagan operated that sounded about right but until she knew for sure, she had to keep him at the top of the list. "Want to tell me about the drug running he operates?"

Freddie shook his head. "I value my life too much."

Alice heaved a sigh. That was all they were going to get out of him. "If at any time you want to talk to me, Freddie, just ring my number. I don't want to release Reagan back onto the streets but without solid evidence I'll have no choice. You can help me with that."

"Sorry, but I've said all I can."

Telling Freddie Whitton he was free to go, Alice remained in the interview room, deep in thought. She'd told him about Sefton's murder — was that a mistake? Probably not. Freddie needed to know what kind of people he was dealing with. At least he'd told her about his mother. Was that important to the case? At this point, Alice wasn't sure but it was another connection and needed to be investigated further.

She was still mulling it over when Hawkes put his head around the door.

"Sefton lived only a stone's throw from where he was found, ma'am. We have his address and I'm organising a forensic search."

"Good. You find anything relating to Reagan and his scams and we've got him. Freddie Whitton is too scared to talk, I'm afraid."

"So, Sefton is all we've got?"

"Him and the two girls, Maggie and Gemma," she said. "And I'd rather Reagan didn't know how important they could be to this case. I need to find that solid piece of evidence and then I'll bring in the girls. Until then we put them somewhere safe and keep quiet about them."

Hawkes wasn't happy. "Unless you come up with something good, he'll walk."

"Yes, and there's nothing I can do about it."

"When d'you intend to interview him?" he asked. "That solicitor of his was back here first thing, bleating on about police harassment."

"We'll give the search party an hour, see what we've got, if anything, and go from there," she said. "How did Wallis and Barrow get on?"

"If they want to go into that cottage, they're going to need a warrant," Hawkes said.

Alice shook her head. "Freddie said his dad was a cantankerous old goat. Okay, tell them to go ahead and organise one. Fiona Whitton knew Reagan. At one time they were an item, so Freddie told me. What d'you make of that?"

"It's yet another connection, ma'am, in a case full of them."

Disheartened, Alice returned to the incident room and made a note on the board. It seemed they were no further forward, despite all the information they were getting. Both cases were no further ahead than yesterday. Later, she'd speak to Louise Morley again, make it more formal. Maybe there was more the girl could tell her, and that could make all the difference.

CHAPTER TWENTY-EIGHT

Back in her office, Alice rang Dr Jack Nevin, their senior forensics man. "Jack, I'm desperate. I need something to keep Max Reagan under lock and key. Have you got anything that'll give me a few extra hours?"

"Well, we found drugs on his business premises and I have a team searching his house. We'll be using the dogs there too. We get anything, I'll ring you straight away."

That would have to do for now but time was getting on, and that solicitor of Reagan's was hovering in the wings. The minute the twenty-four hours were up, he'd have his client out. "What about the shooting in Ardwick, got anything on that?"

"My people are searching the victim's flat now," Nevin said. "We get anything on that one too, I'll let you know. Unfortunately, there is no CCTV in that alley so we're having to rely on the cameras in the adjoining footpath and the road."

Meanwhile, the clock was ticking. "I need something more than just my suspicion if I'm to hang onto him, Jack."

"We're working flat out, Alice, we can't go any faster."

Alice had no choice but to wait for the inevitable. She went back into the incident room and studied the board.

Reagan was one thing but they also had the murders of four young girls to solve. Was Reagan responsible for those too? And what about this other person Louise Morley had told her about, the main man in the drugs world in her day. Had he got something to do with it, or was this too much of a leap? At least they now had names for the victims and that was something, she supposed.

They also had more than one suspect — namely Reagan, the Kendrick family and one unknown. What they didn't have was a motive for any of the suspects. According to Freddie, Reagan didn't kill his own people unless they crossed him. So, what was his motive? Was the murder of the girls something to do with his takeover of the enterprise?

She was staring at the board when Roger Wallis came to tell her that the warrant for the search of Whitton's cottage had come through. "Want me to organise a team, ma'am?"

"You, Barrow and me. The three of us will take a look. I want to see for myself whether he's as obnoxious as Freddie said he was. Plus the drive will give me time to think. We'll go after I've interviewed Reagan."

"And, ma'am, Whitton has a dog, a vicious bugger from the sound of him. We may need a dog handler."

Busy sifting through her paperwork, Alice nodded absently. "Leave that with me."

She was not looking forward to the Reagan interview, not without something to throw at him. She desperately needed Jack and the search team to come up with the goods.

Wallis noticed the addition she'd made to the board regarding Reagan and Fiona. "You don't think he's our killer, do you?"

"I'm not sure what to think," Alice said wearily. "A bullet through the brain is more Reagan's style, so I'm told. As Sergeant Hawkes pointed out, what was done to those girls is far too complex, too ritualistic to be him."

"If Reagan knew Fiona Whitton, that means he must have heard about the Kendricks. I wonder what his take on them was."

She smiled at Wallis. "I'll be sure to ask when I interview him."

* * *

Alice and Hawkes were making their way along the corridor to the interview room. "This could well be a monumental waste of time," she said. "We have very little on him. Granted, drugs were found on his premises and there is what Maggie and Gemma told us, but we have no evidence that he had anything to do with the murdered girls. Which means that everything we have got, everything we've been told, still isn't enough to take to the CPS. Stubbs, that solicitor of Reagan's, is dynamite. You wait, before we know it he'll have half a dozen witnesses to testify that the girls are the guilty ones, and that they hid the drugs and were responsible for distributing them. Which in a sense is perfectly credible — that gym of his is open to the public and half the lockers don't even have keys."

"It's almost as if he'd prepared in advance for something like this."

Hawkes could be right. "Either way, this won't be pleasant. That solicitor will give us both barrels. I can feel the pain now."

"Chin up, ma'am. We've sorted harder cases than this one."

He was talking Still Waters and he was right. "I want Reagan, Sergeant, just as much as I wanted Mad Hatter. I want him banged to rights with no room to wriggle out of it. Now, how d'you reckon we do that?"

Jason Hawkes shrugged his broad shoulders. "We need forensic evidence. That, or the search to throw up something concrete."

"Easy to say, but can Jack come up with the goods?"

* * *

Upon entering the room, Alice and Hawkes were met with an irate solicitor and one amused detainee. The smug look on Reagan's face was almost more than she could take.

"I do hope you've got evidence of wrong-doing to justify keeping my client all this time," Stubbs said. "And unless that folder you're clutching so tightly contains enough to arrest him, we're out of here."

"Calm down, Dominic," Reagan said. "I'm sure the detective knows what she's doing and I have no objection to helping the police — although I do draw the line at spending another night in a cell. Those beds are torture."

Alice glanced at her mobile. Nothing from Jack. "We found a quantity of drugs in some of the lockers at your gym. Any idea how they got there?"

Smiling, he spread his hands. "What can I say? Some of my customers have problems. I do try but I can't help everyone."

"You are aware of the way my client runs his gym, so you know full well that anyone could have left those drugs."

Alice wanted to throttle the solicitor. She dearly wanted to point out that they also had the testimony of the girls but she dare not. Doing that would simply add to the danger they were already in.

"Okay," she allowed. "For now, we will agree that the drugs could have got into those lockers without your knowledge, Mr Reagan."

"Not could, *did*," the solicitor said at once.

Glaring angrily at him, she continued to address Reagan. "I believe you knew Fiona Whitton, Freddie's mother?"

Reagan shook his head. "You're not pinning that one on me too. I'm perfectly well aware that she's missing, but her disappearance has nothing to do with me."

"I didn't say that it did," retorted Alice. "I simply want to know a little more about her — what made her tick, who her friends were."

"Fiona had little opportunity to socialise or make friends. Her tyrant of a husband kept her on a tight leash. She hated him, that much I do know. She wasn't too keen on those brothers of hers either, money-grabbing misers that they are. Have you been to that factory of theirs? It's like something from the dark ages. They treat their staff that way too — low wages, crap conditions and no avenues to voice their complaints. Express a negative opinion and you're out." He shook his head. "I'm not surprised Fiona left, I just wonder why she didn't do it sooner."

"Albert Whitton doesn't work at that factory. What was his opinion of the brothers?"

"I've no idea. I've never met Albert and I only know him by reputation. He's a fool. He let a good woman go because he prefers to live like a hermit. There was certainly no love lost between them. In my opinion, Fiona did the right thing. She'll have gone as far away from him and his vicinity as possible, and I don't blame her."

He appeared genuinely outraged on her behalf, not something Alice had seen in Reagan before. Perhaps he really did feel for Fiona and was pleased she'd got away. "Has she contacted you?" she asked. "And don't lie, because we can check your phone records."

Reagan shook his head. "No. Not even to say goodbye. And before you ask, yes, that cut deep. I believed that me and Fiona had a future together, I thought we were close. But it seems I was wrong. She didn't want me, all she really wanted was her freedom."

This was another side of Reagan. Here was a man who genuinely felt for someone and missed her enormously. Alice took a deep breath. Now for the biggie. "D'you know a girl called Ellie Fleming, a teenager from the Langdale? Rumour has it she worked as a runner for you."

Alice noticed the way Reagan's jaw tightened. He wasn't so relaxed now. "What are you trying to pin on me now, Inspector? Well, it won't work. I never met the girl and you've no evidence that I did. Apart from which, I'm not in the drugs business, so what would I need runners for?"

"Four girls, all from the Langdale and all murdered in horrific ways. Ring any bells?"

"If you have evidence of any wrongdoing on my client's part, please present it, otherwise I must insist you put an end to this particular line of questioning."

Alice looked at Reagan. She must have touched a nerve because he'd gone quite grey in the face. "Are you okay?"

He swallowed. "A bad memory." She waited but he didn't elaborate.

CHAPTER TWENTY-NINE

Alice, with Roger Wallis beside her, was in the back of one of two cars making their way to Albert Whitton's cottage. The other car carried four uniformed officers.

"He lives a bit far out, ma'am," Barrow said from behind the wheel. "His cottage is on a dirt track in the hills beyond Hollingworth Lake."

Alice knew the area. It was rugged, the roads were poor, and if it snowed in winter you were goosed. It wasn't much use living up here without transport either, there were no buses. Not her style at all. Alice liked the freedom living close to the city centre brought with it. If the car gave her problems, she could jump on a bus or a tram and still get to work on time.

"That's it over there." Barrow pointed. "The stone cottage surrounded by the field with the three outbuildings strung along the bottom."

"We make sure to look at those closely," Alice said. This was a lonely spot, perfect for keeping someone hidden away from prying eyes. Your victim could scream their lungs out and no one would hear. It wasn't far from Ravenswood either. A lot could go on here and no one'd be any the wiser.

Her mobile rang, it was Hawkes with the unwelcome news that Reagan had walked. "As soon as his allotted time was up, his solicitor escorted him off the premises."

"Did he say anything?" she asked.

"A few choice words. He doesn't want us bothering him again. When I said I couldn't promise that, Reagan almost lost it. His solicitor only just managed to calm him down."

Alice gave a deep sigh. This wasn't how she'd wanted it to be. Reagan should have been charged and put before a magistrate. There was still a question mark over his involvement with the dead girls, and then there was the drug dealing.

"We're here, ma'am," Barrow said.

He parked among the weeds in front of the house and they got out. Wallis banged on the door and they heard the dog barking inside but no Whitton. The seconds ticked by. Either Whitton was out or he was choosing not to open the door.

"Well, since we have a warrant we might as well start with the outbuildings," Alice said.

She beckoned to the uniformed officers and directed them to search the buildings. "Turn them inside-out. If you find any indication that the girls were held here, we'll get a forensic team on the job."

The officers, along with Barrow, had just started to walk towards the buildings when the cottage door swung open.

A huge German Shepherd dog leaped out and lunged at her. Alice, however, was unfazed. She took a treat from her pocket and held it out to the beast. "Hello, boy. Want one of these?" She scratched him behind his ears.

The dog gave a little whimper and licked her hand. She smiled up at Whitton. "There we are. Friends for life."

"What d'you lot want now?" he asked. "I told you I wasn't having any. You can't come in here and that's an end to it."

"That's where you're wrong, Mr Whitton. We have a search warrant — see?" Alice held it out.

He marched up to Alice and wagged a finger in her face. "You think you're so clever, don't you? Coming here with treats for the dog. Well, that doesn't impress me."

"It impresses him though," Alice said as Wolf raised a paw, begging for a second treat.

Whitton yanked the dog away. "I'll lock him in the kitchen. Be sure to leave everything as you found it. I find anything out of place and I'll sue."

Snapping on a pair of gloves, Alice pushed past him. "We'll start upstairs," she told Wallis. Turning to Barrow, she poured a handful of treats into his palm. "Stay down here and keep an eye on him—" she nodded toward Whitton — "and make sure that poor dog comes to no harm."

Where to start? The place was a tip. It was obvious that no one had done any cleaning in months. There were three bedrooms, only one of which looked used — Whitton's, she presumed. Gingerly, she checked the bedsheets — not Kendrick's.

Downstairs was even worse if possible. The kitchen sink was full of dirty crockery and pans. A rusty old Aga with rotting food stuck to the hob took up half the floor space and heaps of empty tins littered the windowsill. Flies buzzed about the debris, making Alice wince. The place was a disgrace.

"D'you have a cellar?" Alice asked.

Another filthy look. "Why? There's nowt down there."

"Just open it, Mr Whitton," she said.

He took a set of four keys from a hook in the kitchen, stuck one in the lock and stood back. "Help yourself and watch the cobwebs. I've not been down there in years."

Alice called to Wallis and cautiously they descended a steep flight of stone steps.

"Bloody dangerous these," Wallis commented. "One slip and you've broken your neck."

At the bottom of the steps a single lightbulb hung from a cord. Alice felt for the switch on the wall and was relieved to find that it still worked. Whitton had been right to warn of the cobwebs. The place was festooned with them. She watched a large spider scurry off into a dark corner. There was nothing down here, not a stick of furniture, nothing. It was obvious that no one had ventured down here in ages.

Wallis was checking his mobile. "It looks like the cottage is clear, ma'am, the lads haven't found a thing. They've also drawn a blank with the outbuildings."

Disappointed again. Alice sighed. They badly needed a break, anything at all to point them in the right direction. Still, Whitton had been an outside chance. The betting was still on Reagan.

The pair climbed back up to the kitchen. Whitton was waiting for them, keys in hand. "Can't risk anyone accidentally stumbling down them stairs. Could be lethal." He gave them a wicked grin.

"Is that what happened to your wife?" Alice asked, and bit her tongue. The words were out before she could stop them.

"You've got me all wrong," Whitton said. "My wife and I split amicably. We discussed it and agreed it was for the best. I even paid money into her account for a few weeks after."

"I've heard quite a different story," Alice said. "So has Freddie."

"The lad's an idiot and a drug addict," he said. "I wouldn't trust a word he says."

The uniformed officers had finished and were ready to leave. "Amicable or not, we still can't locate Fiona. Can you help clear that up?" she asked Whitton.

"No. She walked out and that was that. No phone calls, no letters, nothing. She just disappeared. I haven't seen her in two years. Neither have those brothers of hers, or so they say. They're a couple of dodgy buggers if you ask me."

Alice wouldn't describe them quite like that. The brothers were certainly odd and old-fashioned, but dodgy? "What makes you call them dodgy?"

"They're always out for themselves, particularly that Felix. They reckon they sell top notch goods but I know they cut corners. They threaten suppliers and withhold payment. Fiona used to work in the office with Ralph. She saw firsthand how they operated. Brothers or not, she had no time for either of 'em."

Interesting, but without anyone to back up this story, it was simply hearsay. She turned to leave. "Thank you for your help, Mr Whitton. We may need to speak to you again. If we do, we'll ring first."

CHAPTER THIRTY

It was the eyes that bothered him. They followed him around the room, staring at him accusingly. Eyes that said they knew what he'd done. Enraged by their stares, he took a felt tip pen and drew a large red cross over four of the photos pinned on the wall. They had no right to judge him. As far as he was concerned, these four deserved everything they got. He'd done well.

He clutched at his chest, wheezing. Was it the cold in this place that had brought it on? Or was it the stress of the investigation and his efforts to avoid it? Another problem had presented itself of late — the appointment of a new senior officer to the case. He picked up the new photo from the table and pinned it on the board along with the others.

"Be careful, Alice," he said, addressing it. "Don't interfere with my work. If you're not too clever I might let you live."

Might. He didn't have much time for the police, most of them were fools. But this one had a reputation. She would need watching.

His gaze moved to the photo beside Alice's. He still had her to find and deal with before the business was done. Get rid of her and he could finally rest. He'd close up this place, walk away and never look back. Simple — except that it wasn't. He had no idea where to find her. Unlike the others, she hadn't stayed in the locality.

The four he'd dealt with had been easy to find. A question here, a face spotted in town and he'd soon got what he needed. But his remaining victim was a different matter. Finding her would take work. His only hope was the fact that a relative of hers who lived in the town was ill. If he was lucky, she'd visit and he'd grab his chance. If not, he'd have to cast the net wider.

His latest victim, the troublemaker, had been on TV and in the paper. The police had found her body and were investigating her death. This had bothered him at first. It was too soon, the lime hadn't had time to do its work. Even so, they had little chance of identifying her. He'd been careful. The scrawny body would tell them nothing.

Would the police link this killing to the others? Possibly, but they could be stupid at times. More often than not they took the easiest route. A mistake, but then that was the police all over. They'd issued a warning on the local news, telling young girls out alone at night to be careful. Meaning they assumed his victims were chosen at random.

Whereas there was nothing random about it at all. But what did they know?

He locked the door to the dark, cramped room and its horrific memories and climbed the stone steps to the ground floor. The effort, along with the icy cold of the cellar, brought on a fit of coughing. Bent double, he staggered to the sink and spat out a gob of blood. Once this was done, he'd take a holiday somewhere warm and put the memory of these last few years behind him.

CHAPTER THIRTY-ONE

It had been a long, hard day. Back at the station, Alice grabbed a quick coffee, gathered her things and prepared to set off for home. She planned to spend the evening reading through the file again just in case there was something she'd missed. With the file in her bag and her mobile stashed in her jacket pocket, she was about to go out of the door when Jason Hawkes stuck his head in. His expression was grim.

"The house we put the Hewsons and the others in has been firebombed, ma'am. The emergency services are in attendance but we've no details as yet."

Alice groaned. Just what she'd been desperate to avoid. "What about Louise Morley, was she with them?" Seeing the uncertainty on his face, she said, "You'd better get someone round to her grandmother's in Droylsden just in case. And I thought that was a safe house we put them in. Only certain members of the team knew where it was, so what happened? How did Reagan find out?"

"We can't be certain this was down to Reagan," he said. "But if we're going with the theory that it was, then we have to assume someone told him."

That made Alice shiver. If that was the case, Freddie Whitton had been right and they did have a spy in the team.

One of her people was working for Reagan, passing on information and happily putting innocent people at risk.

"Hawkes," she called to him. "Come in and close the door."

He sat down opposite her.

"You know what I'm going to ask, don't you?" she said. "Who do you think it is? Which one of the team has been giving out information to a killer?"

Hawkes shrugged. "The thing is, we've not known them very long, so it's difficult to point the finger. I'm not keen on Barrow, for instance, but he does get the job done."

Alice nodded. She too disliked Barrow. "What do we know about him?"

"Not a lot. He's not given to gossip. I know nothing of his private life other than that he's a regular at the Beaufort Arms down the road, and often goes there after work."

"I know you've got enough on your plate already, but could you watch him? Turn up at the pub, buy him a drink and see who he talks to. Check the place out too. I'd like to know who owns it."

Alice had an idea that they were up against a gangster who didn't want anything to threaten his position. If he found out that someone in Alice's team had a weakness and the opportunity presented itself, he wouldn't hesitate to exploit it.

"If this is down to Reagan, he could have guessed that the most likely grasses were the girls, or failing them, Freddie. It's not much of a leap to take," Hawkes said.

Alice shook her head. Hawkes was wrong. Freddie worked for Reagan, and as far as he was concerned, was on his side. Plus Reagan still held a candle for Fiona, Freddie's mother. Added to which, once he found out what had happened to Sefton, Reagan would know full well that Freddie wouldn't dare cross him. The girls, on the other hand, were a different story.

"Reagan knew the address of that safe house. Someone here had to have told him. There are only a few of us in the team who know about it, so it has to be one of us. They've been keeping Reagan in the picture all along, they've told him about the girls and what they'd said about him. How else would he know where we've put them?"

"Once we find out, we'll need proof if we're to use it, ma'am," Hawkes said.

He was right, of course, but first they had to identify him. "Meanwhile, we'd better get round to the house, see what's happened. I only hope to God no one has been badly hurt."

Alice's mobile rang. It was DC Tony Birch, who was attending the incident along with a couple of uniformed officers.

"I'm at the safe house, ma'am. Andrew Hewson has suffered superficial burns and his daughter smoke inhalation. Both are currently in the Oxford Road infirmary. The others are okay. The house is in a right state. They won't be able to go back there for some time."

"Has anyone spoken to them?"

"They were being taken away in an ambulance when I turned up. The daughter, Maggie, told me she saw a black estate car cruising up and down the road before the explosion. She'd gone into the kitchen at the back of the house to tell her dad when the fire started. The senior fire officer says white spirit was poured through the letterbox, followed by a lit taper. Not content with that, a bottle containing a flammable liquid was thrown in through the sitting room window. They were lucky, all things considered. Both Hewson and his daughter escaped out of the back and into the garden. The injuries Hewson suffered were down to him trying to rescue the cat."

"And did he?"

"Yes, ma'am. Maggie's kitten is safe and well."

Alice turned to Hawkes. "A black estate. Any ideas?"

"Maggie got a partial registration," Tony Birch said. "She's a resourceful girl, she knew it could be useful."

"I'll pass it on to the team. They might get something. Hawkes and I will be with you shortly." She turned to her sergeant. "After we've been to the house, we'll visit the Hewsons in hospital."

On the way out she handed Barrow the piece of paper with the registration number. "Get that checked out, a black estate car. You find out who it belongs to, ring me on my mobile." Alice didn't tell Barrow where she and Hawkes were going.

"I want the Hewsons watching night and day," she said to Hawkes in the lift. "I do not want to give the likes of Reagan a second chance, d'you understand?"

Hawkes nodded. "Ma'am, don't you think it was a mistake to have Barrow looking for that car? Given what we suspect, I mean."

"We'll see what comes of it. When we get back, you can have a look yourself, compare your results with Barrow's. Anyone in there asks—" she nodded at the incident room — "we have no idea how the Hewsons are — they're safer if Reagan thinks the attack was successful."

* * *

The burned-out building, now a smouldering wreck, was one of a row of detached houses in Didsbury. Alice stood for a moment, staring at the remains of their safe house. Whoever had done this wanted the Hewsons dead, that much was obvious.

One of the firefighters strode towards them. "You can't stand there, it's not safe."

Alice showed him her badge. He introduced himself as Rod Harper, the senior firefighter. "It'll take some work to put that little lot right," he said, picking up pieces of debris and throwing them aside.

"Do we know for sure how it started?" Alice asked.

"I will do a full report but from our initial findings it looks like the seat of the blaze was the mat behind the front door. An accelerant was poured through the letterbox and set alight. It'll be tested, of course, but it smells like white spirit to me. Then just to be sure, a lit bottle of accelerant was thrown through the front window."

Alice looked at Hawkes. "Whoever did this wanted the Hewsons dead, and the only person currently in the frame is Reagan."

Alice thanked Rod Harper and returned to her car. "I'm off to the hospital, but you can get off home if you want. I'll drop you at the station. I know tomorrow is Saturday but I'd like you in. And don't forget about Barrow. A trip to the Beaufort Arms would be a help."

Hawkes nodded. "No probs, ma'am. Me and Beth have had a talk and she understands about the job a bit better now."

* * *

Andrew Hewson was being kept in overnight. Both his hands were bandaged and the front of his hair was singed.

"It looks worse than it is," he said.

"And Maggie?" Alice asked.

"She's a lot better. She's gone with your officer to get some drinks. If she hadn't spotted that car driving up and down the road, we'd have been toast."

"I'll arrange for Maggie, Gemma and her family to go to a different safe house," Alice said.

Hewson looked doubtful. "With respect, this safe house business doesn't seem all that safe. We were only there five minutes before the place was attacked."

"We're looking into that," she said. "We have a good idea of what happened."

"Is this down to that gangster Maggie spoke about?" he asked.

"We think so, but nothing is certain yet. Rest assured, you won't be left alone. If whoever attacked you tries again, we'll be waiting."

CHAPTER THIRTY-TWO

Jason Hawkes rang his wife, Beth, from the station car park to tell her he'd be late home. His intention was to go along to the Beaufort Arms pub and do a little research. If what had happened to the Hewsons was down to Barrow passing information to Reagan, they needed to know.

Despite being in the centre of Manchester, the pub wasn't busy. Hawkes put that down to it being early on a Friday night. No doubt the place would fill up later. The handful of men loitering at the bar took no notice of Hawkes as he wandered over. Nor did the couple eating at the window table, who were too wrapped up in each other to notice anyone. After a quick glance around the room, Hawkes went over to the bar and ordered a half of bitter. He'd spotted a camera pointed towards the customers and stood well to the side of it.

"Not seen you in here before," the barman said. "We've got a turn on later, a singer. He usually goes down well."

"Afraid I'll have to miss it," Hawkes said. "This is just a quick one after a heavy day."

"D'you work local then?" the barman asked.

"I'm a solicitor," Hawkes lied. "I work for that firm next to the cop station. It's a handy place to be because they put a lot of work our way."

"We get a lot of cops and detectives in here," the barman said. "They can be a rowdy lot too. Surprising, considering the job they do."

"I'm working with one of them at the moment, a detective in CID. I must say I'm not finding him too friendly. He's uncooperative, doesn't tell me what I need to know and that's hindering the case."

The barman laughed. "Got something to hide, has he? Believe me, he's not the only one."

"You could be right. I don't know that much about him as yet." Hawkes took a photo of Barrow from his pocket and handed it over. He was taking a chance, for all he knew the barman could be Barrow's best pal. "You may be able to help me there. Does he ever come in here?"

The barman took the photo from him. "Oh yeah, that's Neil. He's in CID, works on some high-profile cases. Look, mate, word in your ear. Don't get on the wrong side of that one. He's got some dangerous friends."

"Is that so?" Hawkes said. "Well, that's bad news. I've got to ask him some tricky questions tomorrow about a murder he's investigating. Some poor bloke who got himself shot."

The barman leaned forward. "I know he's a detective and they have to mix with some bad types, but I have seen him drinking in here with the big man himself."

Hawkes shot him a puzzled look. "Big man? Who's that then?"

"None other than Max Reagan. You must know him, the drug dealer who currently runs Manchester. If you ask me, Reagan's got the entire CID in his pocket."

"The police?" Hawkes asked. "What, the lot of them?"

"Take my word for it. Neil and that Reagan have something going on. You should see them in here, heads together like bosom pals." He glanced around. "I reckon Neil passes stuff on — you know, tells Reagan what the police are up to and if they're getting too close."

"Blimey," Hawkes said. "I had no idea. I bet he gets well paid for his trouble."

"More than that. Reagan has something on him."

"You don't say. I'm intrigued." This time Hawkes wasn't lying.

The barman smiled. "I'm in here most of the time and I notice what goes on. Barrow gambles, you see. He comes in here every spare minute he has and each time he spends at least a ton on those fruit machines we've got."

So that was it. Barrow had a gambling habit and it looked like Reagan was paying for it. In return, Neil Barrow was passing on vital information.

Hawkes drained his beer and left the pub. On his way home, he pulled into a lay-by and rang Alice.

"I'm just turning into my drive," she said. "I thought you were off home an hour ago."

"I went to the Beaufort Arms for a quick one, ma'am. It was certainly worthwhile. For instance, I discovered that Barrow gambles, he spends a fortune most nights. So, you might wonder, where does the money come from?"

"Go on, give me a clue. It's been a long day and my poor brain can't work it out."

"The barman told me that he's seen Barrow in there drinking with Reagan."

That was bad news indeed. Alice had been hoping they were wrong about Barrow. "Oh dear, now we do have a problem. Good work, Hawkes. Now get off home, I don't want Beth on my tail for working you too hard. We'll discuss what to do about Barrow in the morning."

CHAPTER THIRTY-THREE

Briefcase in hand, Alice locked the car and made for her front door. She was halfway through when she heard a noise coming from the kitchen. It sounded like the clatter of crockery.

"It's only me," Dilys sang out. "I thought I'd make myself useful and fix you something nourishing as you're working so hard."

Alice's pounding heart slowed but she was still surprised. What about Dilys's sister? Wasn't Dilys supposed to be grieving? And what about the funeral and all that?

Dilys appeared in the kitchen doorway, drying her hands on a tea towel and smiling brightly. "I bet you've had nothing to eat all day. You haven't, have you?"

Closer up, Alice saw the tell-tale signs on her face — the too-bright smile and the eyes puffy from crying. "A cup of tea will do me for now. I'll make it. Why don't you go and sit down."

But Dilys brushed her aside. "I need to keep busy, it takes my mind off things."

"It won't work," Alice said. "I know from experience. When I lost my parents, I tried to bury myself in all sorts of stuff, particularly work, but grief has a habit of catching up on you."

Dilys's lip trembled. Alice's words had hit home.

Dilys burst into tears. "I can't go back to my house on my own, it's too . . . too painful. She lived next door, you know, our Doris. I saw her every day and we told each other everything. I'm going to miss her so much. It was only living near her and doing for you that kept me sane."

Alice put her arms around her. "You don't have to go home. Why don't you stay here with me? I'll be glad of the company, to be honest. I spend too much time on my own with my face stuck in some file or other. There's a room upstairs with your name on it, and it's yours for as long as you need."

Dilys shook her head. "That's very kind of you, Alice, but you don't want me cluttering up your life."

Alice kissed her cheek. "I'd love to have you cluttering up my life, Dilys. And it'll make me feel so much better knowing that you are here."

Dilys gave her a genuine smile. "I'll finish making our supper then."

"No, leave it," Alice said. "You've done enough. I'll send out for something — how about a pizza?"

"I've never had pizza delivered before," Dilys admitted. "It's not the sort of thing I usually go for. But it won't matter this once."

Supper sorted, Dilys seemed a bit brighter. Alice could only hope that it lasted.

Alice took the cup of tea Dilys handed her and went through to the sitting room. She put the case file on the coffee table, it was unlikely she'd get round to it tonight. Dilys needed her.

"We can go round later and collect your things," Alice offered.

"Stay away for too long and I might not want to go back," Dilys admitted.

Alice smiled. "Don't let that worry you. You'll probably feel different once you've had time to process what's happened."

The front doorbell rang. "That'll be the pizza," Alice said getting to her feet. "We'll eat and then call it a day. You look done in and I'm shattered."

"Are you working tomorrow?" Dilys asked once Alice came back into the kitchen, pizza boxes in hand.

Alice nodded. "We've got a nasty murder and the rest to sort, so I'll be busy for a while yet. Are you sure you'll be okay?"

"I'll be fine. I'll sort that back bedroom and do a little gardening."

Alice knew that once Dilys felt better, there would be no stopping her. She smiled to herself. All she could do was help her over this bad phase in her life.

Just as they were about to sit down to eat, her mobile rang, it was Roger Wallis. "Whitton did make payments to his wife after she left him. Six in all, two hundred pounds a time. The money hasn't been touched, ma'am. Given that Fiona Whitton is simply missing no one else can touch it either."

So her husband had been telling the truth. Was he likely to pay money into the account of a woman he knew to be dead? Alice didn't think so.

CHAPTER THIRTY-FOUR

Saturday

"What d'you want to do about Barrow, ma'am?" Hawkes asked as soon as he spotted Alice coming in.

"Has he offered up any information about the black car Maggie Hewson saw on the street?"

"Not yet, but I've done a few checks and found this." He handed her a sheet of paper. "Spotted on CCTV two streets away and the registration has the letters Maggie told us about."

"Who does it belong to?"

"It's registered to Reagan's gym," Hawkes said.

"And finding this info took you how long?"

"No more than an hour, ma'am. Barrow should have found something for you by now."

Alice looked across to the DC's desk. He had his head down working on something but didn't appear to be in any hurry.

"DC Barrow. That black estate," Alice called. "Got anything?"

"No, ma'am, still looking."

"I'll deal with him later," she told Hawkes. "For now, we've got more important matters to attend to."

Alice called for the team's attention. "Morning, everyone. Today, I want us to go through what we've got and what avenues of enquiry we've yet to investigate." She pointed to Reagan's name on the board. "So far, he's our only suspect, but my instincts tell me different. As Sergeant Hawkes has pointed out, a bullet through the skull is more his style. As far as I'm aware, Reagan has never held girls captive, starved them and tried to disguise their identity after death. Those girls had no hands and no teeth. Whoever is responsible for that did not want us to know who they were. But was that someone Reagan?"

"Could he have been teaching them a lesson? Maybe he was punishing them for crossing him in some way," Wallis said.

"Possibly, but ask yourself, would he really go to all that trouble?" She looked round at their faces, all glued to hers. "Okay, this is your task for the morning. I want Reagan's record going through with a fine toothcomb. I want to know if he's ever done anything remotely like this in the past."

"If it's not Reagan, then who?" Wallis asked.

"Good question," Alice said. "We draw a blank, we look again at the Kendrick family. DC Wallis, you can set up interviews with both brothers in readiness. For my part, I intend to speak to Louise Morley later today. I'm convinced there are things she's not told us. We need to move this on and fast. Time is passing and we're no further ahead." Louise had told her that the boyfriend she'd had, back when she'd worked for Reagan, was a friend of Laser's. "Find Laser too, and bring him in for a chat."

"Are you sure he'll recall anything useful, ma'am? Strikes me the bloke spends most of his time sleeping it off. And neither of the Kendrick brothers are in good health," Hawkes said. "Okay, those girls were worn down by the horrific treatment they suffered, but realistically, both the brothers are so fragile any one of those girls could have overpowered them."

"We don't know that," Alice said. "We know nothing about how they were taken. They might have been drugged, knocked unconscious and been unable to fight back."

Alice picked up the case file and made for her office. "DC Barrow, could I have a word?"

When Barrow sat down in front of her he looked puzzled, not worried.

Alice had decided that there was no point in beating about the bush. "You've been passing information about our current case to Reagan." He opened his mouth to speak but she cut him off. "Don't even consider denying it. I know about the gambling. I presume that's what you needed the money for."

Still, Barrow showed no remorse. "Did Reagan tell you? He's trying it on, ma'am. Surely you see that."

"We have evidence, Barrow. The leak in this team is you."

"I needed the money." Said simply. "And why complain now? Isn't he happy with the information he's getting from me?" Barrow sounded bitter, angry, and so was Alice.

"Why do this, Neil?" she demanded. "Why put lives at risk just to make a few extra pounds? And colluding with Reagan too. You know what that man is like, how he treats people."

"You don't understand," he said. "I was desperate for the money. I was in the Beaufort one night having lost hard on those damn fruit machines. Reagan joined me at the bar when I was drowning my sorrows. He heard me talking about my problems to the barman and offered to help me out. Said it was no biggie and bunged me a couple of hundred. But now he's got me, you see. I'd no idea at the time but he was recording the transaction on his phone. I tried to pay him back but he just laughed. He offered more — Go on, he said, have some fun. I couldn't resist. I have a gambling habit that's not easy to control. Once I start using those fruit machines I can't stop. Reagan knew all about my weakness and exploited it."

"You told him about the safe house and that the Hewsons were there. They could have been killed," Alice said.

"I had no choice. He threated to kill me if I didn't help."

"You could have come to me, told me what was going on. If anyone had been killed, you would have been an accessory to murder, facing a hefty prison sentence. Fancy that instead, did you, Neil?"

Slowly, the realisation of the seriousness of his situation was beginning to dawn on him. "Will this affect my job?"

"I'm afraid so. You will be suspended and denied access to the incident room. I'm not risking the witnesses coming to more harm."

"Please, give me another chance. I can help. I can tell you about Reagan, how he operates, who his people are."

Alice looked at him. Did he really know these things, or was Barrow trying to save his own skin?

"He still uses young people as runners," Barrow said. "I can give you names. Most of them come from the Langdale."

"We can deal with them ourselves. I need a lot more than that if you are to even come close to redeeming yourself."

"He has a right-hand man to iron out any problems that come his way," Barrow said.

"Sefton, we know."

"No, not him, someone else."

Now Alice was interested. "Go on."

"He uses a man called Denny, Patrick Dennison."

CHAPTER THIRTY-FIVE

Within the hour Alice had told the rest of the team that Barrow was no longer working with them, although she didn't explain why. She'd also informed Superintendent Leo Monk.

He shook his head. "I brought him into the team myself. Has he done much damage?"

"Enough. I certainly don't want him back."

"Understood, and don't worry, I'll deal with him. How is the case going?"

How to answer that one? She gave him the stock response. "We're following several leads, sir." It would have to satisfy him. After all, he hadn't fared much better when he was in charge of the case.

"I'm sorry about this, Alice. I had hoped the team would be more supportive, give you the help you need."

"I've got Hawkes and Wallis, and some of the others are okay. Barrow was the exception, I hope. However, he did give me one useful piece of information."

"A last-ditch attempt to redeem himself, I suppose," Monk said. "Well, keep me posted, won't you?"

She left Monk to it and went back to the team. Barrow had cleared his desk and the gossip had already started, something she needed to put a stop to quickly.

"New information," she called to the team. "It appears that Reagan has a right-hand man hitherto unknown to us. One Pat Dennison, known on the street as Denny."

There was a murmur around the room. The name was obviously familiar to a few of them. "I want a full history of this Denny and his current whereabouts if known. If the man's as dangerous as I've been told, what's he doing on the loose?"

"Can I ask who supplied this information, ma'am," Roger Wallis said.

Alice looked at him. It was no use lying. The rumour mill would reveal all soon enough. "Neil Barrow."

"And he's a reliable source?" Wallis sounded sceptical. "You're sure he's not just thrown this name into the pot to get you into bother? Dennison hates all things police. He's been on an assault charge for clobbering a uniformed officer before now."

"Despite what you may think, this time Barrow genuinely was trying to help."

Wallis shrugged. "Okay, we'll research the man, see what we come up with."

"When you've got something, let me know." Alice made herself a quick coffee and retired to her office. The name Dennison hadn't come up before and added a whole new dimension to the case. How did he operate? Was he a bullet-in-the-head type, or would he take the time to make his victims suffer like those girls did?

One strong coffee later, Alice picked up her phone and rang Louise Morley. "We need to speak today."

"I'm busy. Anyway, I doubt I can tell you anything more than I already have," Louise said.

Alice wasn't going to be fobbed off. "Not even if I consider you to be in grave danger?"

"I don't believe you. Last night I was out with my gran. We were in the pub on the Langdale and I bumped into Reagan. He seemed perfectly pleasant, bought us a drink and shared a joke with Gran. I don't think he wants me dead at all."

"Nevertheless, I still want to speak to you. Reagan might be the least of your problems," Alice said, thinking of Dennison. "I have your address and I'll be round within the hour."

Alice put the receiver down and opened the case file. Four girls and Louise. Why was she the only one left alive? The question had been bugging her since they'd first met. She had a grandmother who lived locally. It wouldn't have been that hard to find her if the killer really wanted to.

Hawkes stuck his head round her door. "Want the low-down on Dennison?"

"Interesting, is it?"

"He is one slippery character that's for sure. Nothing sticks. By rights he should have been locked up tight years ago. Robbery with violence, not to mention suspected murder."

"Who?"

"A former henchman of Reagan's who crossed him. He was found floating in the Rochdale canal with a bullet through his heart having been badly beaten first. Dennison was the main suspect but nothing was ever proved."

"And?" Alice asked. Hawkes had a look on his face that smacked of him knowing more.

"The victim had had his hands cut off and his face smashed in."

Alice got to her feet. "Know where to find him? I think we need a word."

"Currently he's helping out at Reagan's gym," Hawkes said.

"Did the case get to court?" she asked.

"There wasn't enough evidence, so the CPS threw it out."

"We'll have a word with him, get a feel for what he's about, and then I want to speak to Louise Morley. There's something she's not telling us and it could be important."

CHAPTER THIRTY-SIX

When she and Hawkes got to the gym, they were told that Reagan was in the exercise area. They wandered through and spotted him on a treadmill, eyes closed, listening to music through his earphones.

After much waving and calling, Alice managed to attract his attention. Scowling, he snatched out the earbuds. "What? You again? I don't know what more you think I can tell you." He slung a towel around his neck and stalked towards the pair.

"Pat Dennison, what's his position here?"

Reagan shrugged. The name didn't seem to faze him. "General dogsbody. Bloke's been inside so there's a limit to what I can offer. I don't let him handle cash or deal with the youngsters, for example. He's got a short fuse and he's easily tempted — not a good combo. But as I've told you before, I try to help folk."

The smile on his face made Alice want to punch him. What a load of twaddle. Reagan wasn't in the least community-minded. He could put on as big a show as he liked but the fact remained, Reagan was a dangerous, money-grabbing thug who had people killed at the drop of a hat.

"Is he here this morning?" she asked.

"He's showing his girlfriend around." He pointed towards one of the exercise rooms. "Last I saw, they were headed for the Pilates class in there."

Brushing him aside, Alice and Hawkes went across and peered through the large picture window. A class was in progress. Behind them at the back of the room stood a young woman with a man Alice took to be Dennison. But it was the woman who had her attention.

She nudged Hawkes. "Well, I never. What's Louise Morley doing here, I wonder?"

"They look pretty friendly too," Hawkes said. "Dennison — if that is him — has his arm around her waist."

"Well, Reagan did say girlfriend," Alice said. "And when she spoke to me, Louise mentioned having a man in her life, although she didn't say what his name was." She nodded to Hawkes who followed her back to the reception area. "You keep Dennison amused while I have a word with Louise. Don't let him go anywhere. I've got one or two questions to ask that bloke."

Louise saw the detectives beckoning to her through the window, said something to Dennison and came out. "Something up?"

"D'you know him?" Alice asked.

Louise smiled. "Of course I do. He's the boyfriend I mentioned."

"That'd be the one who introduced you to Reagan and got you into running drugs for his customers," Alice said.

Louise bristled. "Denny isn't like that anymore. He's changed. More than that, he's fond of me. Reagan was angry when he spotted me the other night. He knew I'd been speaking to you. I was really frightened but Denny calmed him down, he convinced him I wasn't out to do any harm."

"Back on, is it then, this relationship between you and Dennison?"

Louise nodded. "We've been friends since our early teens. He's okay once you get to know him, not at all like he's made out to be."

Alice sighed. They were setting Louise up for something. "Look, Louise, you're in danger. That's why I allocated you a safe house. Have you given the address to anyone?"

"I couldn't even if I wanted to. I don't know it. The policeman was just going to drive me there when Denny came along and I changed my mind."

That was something at least.

Dennison joined them. "Your oppo says you want a word with me."

Alice gave him a smile and gestured to a table. "Shall we sit down?"

"Going to take a while, is it?" Dennison said with a grin.

"D'you own a black estate car?" Alice asked.

He considered this for a moment. "The gym does and we all get to use it. It's just a general runaround."

"Were you using it yesterday afternoon?" she asked.

"Not sure, I'd have to check the rota."

"Well, do that, please."

Dennison pulled a mobile from the pocket of his hoodie and scrolled through it. "Yes, I was. Why?"

"Okay, in that case where did you go with it?" Alice asked.

"Nowhere special. I don't remember exactly, I probably nipped out to get some fags. I don't like to go missing for long, Max has only recently taken me on and I'm keen to impress. It wouldn't do to go missing on duty in my first few days."

He was being far too glib for Alice's liking. "You sure about that? You weren't heading for the house the Hewson family and others were staying in, by any chance were you?"

"Never heard of them, love. Like I said, apart from ten minutes or so, I was here."

Alice didn't believe him, not for one minute. "Hawkes, can you find out where the CCTV is? The reception area, the gym, whatever they've got. I want to check his story. If he's telling the truth, there should be plenty of footage of his movements. And take that estate car in for a forensic examination."

153

She turned back to Dennison. "Sorry about this, but we have to check your story — procedure, you know."

His air of mild amusement had evaporated. There was now a hard edge to Dennison's voice. "I know how you lot operate. You're trying to fit me up. Well, I've done nothing wrong."

"We're doing nothing of the sort. We don't fit people up," Alice said. "A witness has mentioned your name in connection to an arson attack on a house yesterday."

"Well, your witness is deluded. Like I said, I was here all day. And what witness? If there is one, it'll be someone trying to blacken my name."

For now, they had no grounds for detaining him. "Okay, fair enough, but we'll be speaking to you again," Alice said. "And if I have to come searching it won't bode well for you."

Alice watched Dennison go back into the gym where he had a quick word with Reagan. "You shouldn't trust him," she told Louise. "The man is a crook and he's just out for himself."

"I've known him for ages," Louise said. "He's okay."

"Back when the five of you were working for Reagan, was Dennison involved?"

"Yes, we all were," Louise said.

Alice moved closer to the girl. "Be warned, Louise, that man is dangerous. He's using you. I don't know why but it won't end well for you. Walk away while you can, that's my advice."

CHAPTER THIRTY-SEVEN

"You think Dennison murdered the girls on Reagan's orders?" Hawkes asked.

Alice didn't know what to think. "It's hard to say but it's possible. Dennison has a streak of cruelty in him, we know that. But we have to ask ourselves if he would go to the extent of keeping the girls prisoner before killing them. We mustn't lose sight of that one. We need to find out where the girls were held, and then we might get somewhere. Did you get that CCTV?"

"The manager is emailing it to me."

"Hang around until he does, make sure you get the lot," Alice said. "I don't trust any of them. The manager is employed by Reagan and will do what he says. When you get the film back to base, have a good look at it, along with anything available from around the safe house. What we could really do with is a reasonable look at the driver of that estate car. If he drove up the main road, we might get one."

Hawkes went back into the gym while Alice got into her car and headed for the station. On the way, she got a call from Jack Nevin.

"The search of Sefton's flat has turned up a number of items," he said. "We found half a dozen notebooks in a bin

155

bag of stuff he had stashed under the bedroom floorboards, and they are proving interesting."

"In what way?" she asked.

"Each notebook contains a long list of numbers, dates and amounts of money. I reckon it's a sort of code, but without more information it'll be almost impossible to decipher."

"Why would Sefton be writing stuff in code?" Alice asked.

"I suspect he may have been recording all the drug transactions he carried out for Reagan. But that's mere conjecture on my part."

"Intriguing though. Shame we didn't get to speak to him. Dates and numbers you say."

"So far, but we're still searching the place and for a back street terrace, it rambles a bit."

"Leaving Sefton aside for the moment, have you found anything definitive on the murdered girls?"

"Not yet, we are going over those shrouds again. But I do have something positive to offer on one of the letters sent to Ellie Fleming. We've tested it thoroughly and I can confirm that the paper and ink match the samples from Kendrick's office you gave me. There are no new prints though, just those of the occupants of that flat. Whoever wrote it must have worn gloves."

Alice smacked the steering wheel with her hand. "Kendrick's! I knew it. Thank you, Jack. At last we have something I can use to go after a suspect."

"That's what the Kendricks are, is it, suspects?" he asked.

"Given what you've just told me then yes, I'd say so. We've got your findings from the letter plus the fact that Ravenswood is on their doorstep." She thought for a moment. "D'you have any people spare who could mount a forensic search of Kendrick's factory?"

"Leave it with me. Later today do you?"

"In the meantime, I'll bring the brothers in and meet your team up there at about two."

Alice pulled into the station car park and rang Hawkes from there. "Result. At last Jack has found something. Those letters sent to Ellie were written using Kendrick's paper and ink. We go up there later with a team and search the place thoroughly."

"Well done. Good old Jack," Hawkes said. "I've got all the film from the gym. I'll check it out once I'm back."

Hopeful that they were getting somewhere at last, Alice took the stairs two at a time. She burst into the incident room calling for Tony Birch and Roger Wallis. "I want the two Kendrick brothers bringing in for interview. I doubt they'll give you much trouble but take a couple of uniforms with you in case. Later today, us and Jack Nevin's people will search the Kendrick's factory."

Alice retired to her office and rang home to see how Dilys was. She was unlikely to be back before early evening and was worried about leaving her friend on her own. But she needn't have been concerned. In a cheerful voice Dilys told her she'd spent the morning working in Alice's garden.

"Your Michael rang," she said. "Reckons he'd got some time owed and might get down for a visit."

This was good news. The way things were, she saw precious little of her son, working as he did in Scotland. Promising not to be late, she checked her watch. If she was going to eat, she'd better do it now. Once the interview and search got underway, the day would fly by.

CHAPTER THIRTY-EIGHT

Ralph Kendrick had been brought in and was now seated in an interview room with his solicitor. Observing him through the window, Alice shook her head. Kendrick looked ill, his face was grey and he had a hacking cough.

"What d'you think?" she asked Wallis.

Wallis shrugged. "He's getting on, works too hard and doesn't take care of himself. Simple as that."

Realising she knew nothing about him, Alice asked, "Have we had a look at his private life? Does he have a wife, for instance, or children?"

"No ma'am, there's just him and his brother. Fiona the sister, was the only one who had a child."

"Poor man, from the look of him he could do with a good woman to take care of him. Mind you, in this day and age men should be able to look after themselves, though the task seems to be beyond him. He looks so frail, I hope he doesn't collapse on me. We'd better have the medic standing by just in case."

With the file tucked under her arm and Roger Wallis in tow, Alice entered the room.

"Mr Kendrick," she began, "we have something of a puzzle that we hope you'll be able to help us with. As you know, we found the bodies of several girls buried in the woodland just outside your factory. One of these girls was sent a series of threatening letters. Their evil, abusive content rightly upset the girl. But it was the paper and ink, plus the style in which they were written, that struck me. I realised I'd seen it before."

Alice paused, expecting Kendrick to deny having written any such thing. But he merely shook his head.

"We've had the paper and ink tested and it matches samples I took from your office," she said.

Still, neither Kendrick nor his solicitor said anything.

"Do you have an explanation for that, Mr Kendrick?"

Kendrick glanced at his solicitor who gave a slight nod. "No comment."

"Mr Kendrick, your cooperation at this stage will be to your advantage," Alice said. "You'll only do yourself harm by refusing to speak."

"No comment," Kendrick said again, and dissolved into a prolonged fit of coughing.

"Surely, you can't possibly believe that my client had anything to do with the murder of this girl," the solicitor said.

"Girls," Alice said. "There were more than one of them."

"Mr Ralph's office isn't always locked. He often attends meetings or goes into the workshop. Any number of things takes him away from his office during a normal working day. Anyone wishing to remove some of his writing materials has ample opportunity to do so. What you are accusing my client of will not stand up in court. The fact of the matter is, you have no evidence on which to detain my client."

It was the same story as with Reagan — unlocked doors and sticky fingers. This would get them nowhere.

"I should warn you that I have a warrant to search your factory. We will be visiting your premises later today," she said. "Let's hope for your sake that you're telling the truth, Mr Kendrick."

"I don't lie," he retorted angrily. "Can I go now?"

Alice nodded. "We may need to speak to you again."

* * *

Felix Kendrick could not attend for interview as he'd been carted off to hospital that morning. A frustrated Alice met Hawkes in the incident room. "Why is this happening to us? I had thought the writing materials would be evidence enough to convict Ralph Kendrick, but that solicitor was right. What we have is flimsy at best. As for Felix, he is never well. Ask yourself, could either of them really kidnap those girls, manhandle them, kill them and bury their bodies? Frankly I doubt that either man has the strength."

"I tend to agree, ma'am, but where does that leave us?"

"Precisely nowhere, Hawkes. We'll carry out the search of Kendrick's factory in the interests of thoroughness. We'll go up there first thing on Monday morning, and if we don't find anything we have no choice but to start again."

"What about tomorrow, ma'am?" he asked.

"We take the day off," she said. "I think we all deserve it, don't you?" This case was getting to Alice in ways that she'd not experienced since Mad Hatter. Her only consolation was that she'd seen that through to a successful conclusion. She sat at her desk and flicked through the case file. Their faces stared back at her from the pages. Laser with his cheeky grin; the well-groomed, handsome Freddie. And then there was the likes of Reagan and Dennison. One of them had to be their killer, but which was it?

"Ralph Kendrick and his solicitor have left, ma'am," Hawkes said. "I've made a start with the CCTV and I've roped in Birch to help. He knows how important this is and he won't skip any frames."

"D'you think we're looking at two different cases here, Hawkes?" Alice asked. "I keep asking myself if Reagan and the dealing has anything at all to do with the murder of the four girls."

"But they've got to be connected, ma'am," Hawkes insisted. "All those girls were runners for Reagan and some-one else before him. And they knew Dennison."

"Coincidence perhaps? I've said it before but there is no getting away from it. There are just too many coincidences in this case."

Hawkes nodded. "And that in itself is important, ma'am. After all, coincidence is simply little pieces of evidence that don't appear to fit, but when you have enough of them, they fall into place like pieces in a jigsaw puzzle and suddenly you have the whole picture. That is what will happen here, you'll see."

Alice was not convinced. "I still think we may have two different cases on our hands."

"So why were the girls killed? The obvious explanation is that they crossed Reagan in some way and paid the price," Hawkes said.

He could be right of course, but the way this investigation was going, Alice was inclined to believe that there were quite different motivations behind what had happened.

"Have we found out what happened to Fiona Whitton yet?" she asked.

"No, but it's probable that she's moved out of the area and changed her name. From what we've been told, I can see how she'd want to put the Kendricks and Whitton well behind her."

Alice tapped her pen absently on the desk. "In that case, how do you explain the money? Albert Whitton put cash into her bank account but it hasn't been touched. Why is that, d'you think? I can't get it out of my head that Fiona was unable to touch it because something had happened to her."

"That's pure conjecture, ma'am. We have no evidence either way, and until we get some there's not much we can do."

CHAPTER THIRTY-NINE

Monday

Alice had spent a quiet Sunday with Dilys. They'd cooked dinner together after a leisurely morning spent going through Dilys's wardrobe.

"I need something suitable for the funeral," she sniffed. "Doris didn't much like anything I owned. D'you think I should get something new?"

"If you like, we can nip over to the Trafford Centre next weekend, and see what we can find."

The thought of a shopping trip seemed to cheer Dilys up. "I've not been there in months. I wouldn't mind a look round. Anyway, your breakfast is on the table, and make sure you eat it up. It'll do you good. Will you be home for dinner?"

"I'll try, but don't go to any trouble. That dinner you cooked yesterday will last me most of the week."

"All right," Dilys said, "I'll do something flexible."

Alice said goodbye, climbed into her car and made for the station. When she arrived, there was a full complement, all busy at their desks. The plan was that Wallis and Birch would continue to scrutinise the tapes, while she and Hawkes accompanied the search team to the Kendrick's factory.

They drove off, Alice tutting. "This is a complete waste of time. We've already interviewed Ralph and decided he's unlikely to be guilty, so what are our chances of finding anything useful?"

"At least we'll have covered all bases, ma'am," Hawkes said. "And once Felix is better, we'll interview him too."

All very well, but there were other things they could be doing.

* * *

On arriving at the Kendrick's factory, Alice and the search team joined Jack Nevin and his people.

Mrs Hubble was clearly not happy with the situation. "Mr Ralph wasn't even able to come in this morning. He's upset and hurt that you people think he could be involved in something so awful as the murder of those poor girls."

"Well, I'm sorry, but we have to follow procedure," Alice said.

"Can I ask that your people don't gossip to the staff?" Mrs Hubble said. "The less they know, the better. The rumours are rife as it is."

It was perfectly natural for the staff to be curious about what was going on. Looking around, Alice was immediately aware of the looks and the whispering.

"There's no way either of them men killed anyone," a woman was saying in a low voice as Alice passed her machine. "I've been working here for years. I know them both well and they are not killers."

Alice stopped beside her. "I think you're right, but nonetheless we have to investigate. Anyway, this is about other stuff, not just the murders."

"What other stuff? Tell us and we might be able to help. We're a small close-knit team here, and we usually know what's going on."

As she spoke, a young woman dropped the piece of cloth she'd been checking and bolted towards the ladies.

"Is she all right?" Alice asked.

"Guilty conscience," the woman said.

"What d'you mean?"

The woman looked Alice in the eye. "Light-fingered, that's what she is. Ask her — go on, ask her what she's been doing in Mr Ralph's office."

Alice didn't need telling twice. With a nod to Hawkes, she pointed at the door of the Ladies. "I'll just take a quick peek, find out what's wrong with her."

* * *

Alice found the young woman standing at a sink, dabbing her eyes and obviously in some distress.

"I shouldn't have done it. I told him I was too afraid. I was terrified of getting found out but he wouldn't listen." She looked at Alice, her whole body shaking. "You know, don't you? You know what I did, what I took."

The truth was, Alice hadn't a clue but given the apparent theft of the writing materials, her interest was piqued. "Let's go to the meeting room and you can tell me all about it. What's your name?"

"Trisha Randle."

The meeting room was empty. Alice sat her down and said, "Now Trisha, what have you done that's so awful?"

"I stole some stuff from Mr Ralph's office."

Suddenly, Alice understood. "Would this be some stationery — paper, ink and pens and the like?"

Trisha nodded.

"What did you do that for, Trisha?"

"My boyfriend asked me to get them for him."

"This boyfriend, does he have a name?" Alice asked.

Trisha shook her head. "I tell you that and he'll come after me. I've got kids, I can't risk it."

Alice decided to leave that one for now. "Okay. So, when did he ask you to do this?"

"A while ago. I was to gather the stuff together and hand it over when we next met."

"D'you know what he wanted it for?" Alice asked.

"He said he collected old writing materials. Apparently, there's a ready market for them on the auction sites online, particularly the old fountain pens."

"This is important, Trisha. If we know what his name is it could help us catch a killer. Whereas withholding information could get you into serious trouble, possibly a prison sentence."

But Trisha shook her head. "You don't know him, he's violent. He'll kill me if he knows I told you."

"D'you still see him?" Alice asked.

"We're not going out anymore. We fell out over some money I lent him that he never gave back." She smiled at Alice through her tears. "You must think me a right fool."

"No, but I think you would do well to tell me everything you know. I want his name and I'm prepared to arrest you if you don't give it to me."

That appeared to do the trick. Trisha clutched Alice's arm. "Promise you won't let him come after me. And it's not just him either, he's got some scary friends."

"Tell me who he is and he needn't know it was you who gave it to me."

"I don't know his real name, everyone just calls him Laser."

CHAPTER FORTY

As soon as Alice had obtained a statement from Trisha Randle, she and Hawkes left for the station.

"Laser," she announced to Hawkes. "I could throttle him. He's been playing us all along. He knew what Ellie was up to with Reagan and must have decided to take her to task about it."

"Why would he do that?" Hawkes asked. "Laser's a crook and will do anything for a few quid, but what did he have to gain by sending anonymous letters?"

"I don't know, but it was him who persuaded Trisha Randle to steal the stationary, which we know was used to write all the letters."

"Are you suggesting that Laser killed Ellie and the others?" Hawkes asked. "Because if you are, what would his motive be?"

"I've no idea," Alice said, "but for some reason he wanted to threaten Ellie, and us too at one point. Remember, Ellie wasn't the only one who got letters."

"I suppose he could have been working for Reagan or Dennison, but that's not their style either," Hawkes said doubtfully.

"I want Laser finding and bringing in," Alice said. "And I want some straight answers this time."

Before they set off, Hawkes called the station and alerted the team. With luck they'd pick him up quickly. Alice dearly wanted to know what he had to say for himself. But Hawkes was right to ask about his motive. Why would Laser want to frighten Ellie? More to the point, what had those girls known or seen to get them killed?

* * *

"He reckoned he was expecting us. Brazen about it, he was," said the PC who had brought Laser in. "Mind you, he's off his head on something. He's got that glazed look in his eyes again."

With a nod to Hawkes, Alice took hold of her file and made for the door. "Time to go. Off his head or not, let's see how brazen he is after I've finished with him."

"I've known Laser a while, ma'am. He's a druggie, a con artist who'll do almost anything in order to buy a fix — but murder?" Hawkes shook his head. "I'd never have him down for that."

"Well, perhaps he has hidden talents, Sergeant," she said. To the PC, she said, "Has he asked for a solicitor?"

"Yes, ma'am. The duty one is with him now."

"Good. I don't want him whining on about police malpractice."

Alice and Hawkes made their way to the interview room. "Right, Liam," she began. "It's about time you told us the truth about what you've been up to, and this time I expect you to be straight with us."

Laser turned to his brief with a grin. "*Liam*, eh? She's using my Sunday name, must be serious."

"Oh it is, make no mistake about it. You're here to tell me about the murder of four young girls, one of them being Ellie Fleming."

"Slags, the lot of them," Laser said. "And I know nowt about any murder. You're picking on the wrong person there."

167

He sat back and folded his arms. The self-satisfied look on his face made Alice want to slap him. "Why did you get Trisha Randle to steal for you?"

"I didn't."

"Yes you did. You got her to take certain items of stationery from Ralph Kendrick's office. Those items were used to write several threatening letters to Ellie as well as to my colleagues at the station."

"You couldn't make it up, could you?" Laser chuckled. "This lot are having a right laugh. Threatening letters? Don't they think I've anything better to do?"

"My client is obviously not well," the solicitor said. "He should be examined by a doctor."

"I agree, but he has to talk to me first."

"That accusation you just made — do you have any evidence for that?" the solicitor asked.

"A signed statement from Miss Randle," Hawkes said.

"The letters sent to Ellie spoke of incidents in the past that could have a direct bearing on her death. Tell me about that," Alice said.

Laser thumped the table with his fist. "I've had enough of this crap. It was me who told you about Ellie receiving those letters, if you recall. What's more, I let your officers rifle through my flat until they found the ones I'd kept. If I'm guilty of what you're accusing me of, why would I do that?"

He had a point, Alice had to admit. Why would he indeed? "Whatever the reason, you know something and I want you to tell me what that is."

Laser looked uncomfortable. He shifted around on his chair. Time for his fix? Alice wondered.

"I don't feel right. You've got to let me out." He shook his head. "I've got to see someone. I'm wasting my time in here."

"I'm sorry you don't feel right. Maybe you'll feel better when you've had a chance to think about your position, because you're going to be staying here for a good long while."

"You've got me for twenty-four hours tops. After that you'll have to charge me or let me go."

Alice ignored the comment. "I'll arrange for a doctor to see you, and there'll be an officer nearby so if you need anything, just shout."

Alice stood up. "I want a medic to give him the once over," she said to Hawkes. "He doesn't look great, but he's an expert at fooling us and he knows the law. I want him right. I want him able to speak to us. Then we might actually get somewhere."

CHAPTER FORTY-ONE

His patience had paid off. His last target had returned to the area. At last, he had a chance to silence her for good. It had been a long wait, and he was feeling somewhat nervous. With a full-on police investigation in progress, it wasn't going to be easy. That woman detective had poked her nose in everywhere. Getting the better of her would take finesse and a great deal of luck.

The detective was not the only problem. Louise Morley had some dangerous friends, Patrick Dennison for one, the madman who did Reagan's dirty work. There was no way he wanted to come up against him.

Speed was of the essence. There was no time to plan a strategy. She might talk to someone, tell the police what she knew. If that happened, he was finished. Better to sort the problem quick, before she had time to act.

Louise Morley was staying with her grandmother in Droylsden but she often spent the night at Dennison's flat in Ancoats. He knew that Dennison had given her a key and that she was free to come and go as she pleased. Today, as luck would have it, Reagan was going to look at some new premises in Stockport and was taking Dennison with him.

The pair would be drinking with the vendor until the wee small hours, so this was his chance.

* * *

Alice had her head down checking through the various statements when she heard someone knock on her door. It was the PC who'd been detailed to watch Laser.

"I don't think he's right, ma'am. He's on the deck thrashing around. He's in withdrawal I'd say."

Fine. A spell in hospital and then he'd have to talk to them. There was nowhere else for him to go. They had Trisha's statement, so unless he wanted to be charged himself, he'd have to tell them who he was working for. "Have him taken to hospital, and stay with him. If he says anything at all, I want to know."

"It might help to know what drugs he's on but I doubt he'll tell us that," the PC said.

"We've got something, ma'am." Wallis was standing behind the PC. "We've spotted the black estate on the CCTV footage. It's cruising along the High Street before turning into the road where the Hewsons were staying. And here's the good news. On one frame in particular, you can plainly see that it's Dennison driving."

At last, a step forward. "This is good. I wonder what excuse he'll think up for being there. Have we spoken to the neighbours?"

"Yes, at the time of the fire, but they were all tight-lipped. If they think we're about to arrest someone, things could well change," Wallis said.

Alice nodded. He was right. She picked up the phone and rang Jack Nevin in Forensics. "The black estate from Reagan's gym, have you found anything in it?"

It took a second or two for Jack to respond, during which Alice crossed her fingers and said a little prayer.

"We're out of luck, Alice. The vehicle is clean. No evidence of anything untoward."

Alice found that difficult to believe. "Are you sure, Jack? We've got our suspect on CCTV in the exact area at the right time."

"Look, Alice, I know my job. If I say there's nothing to find, there's nothing to find. And before you ask, the vehicle hasn't been cleaned either. It's actually filthy."

"I'm sorry, Jack. I'm not doubting you, it's just not what I expected."

He laughed. "Don't worry, I won't take it personally."

Putting the receiver down she went with Wallis to see what state Laser was in. The PC and the medic had him in the recovery position.

"He's thrown up all over the cell floor," the PC said. "And he can't stop twitching."

The medic looked up. "I've rung for an ambulance. He needs to be in hospital. I don't know what he's taken but it has to be something pretty potent to leave him in this state."

Alice sighed. "I'm afraid we've had no luck with the black estate," she said to Wallis. "There's no sign of accelerant or any other fire-raising equipment in the boot."

"Are we ruling Dennison out then?" he asked.

Alice spread her hands. Right now she'd no idea what to do about him.

CHAPTER FORTY-TWO

Given that there was no chance of interviewing Laser for several hours at least, Alice decided to bring Dennison in for questioning. She would ask him herself about where he was going in the black estate. She rang the gym, only to be told that he was out with Reagan looking at a property.

Alice was in no mood to be given the run around. "Call him," she told the assistant at the gym. "Tell him to come in to Manchester Central at once, or I'll have him arrested."

She put the phone down, rested her elbows on the desk and pushed her hair back off her face. Everywhere she looked in this case there were hold-ups. Nothing was simple. She badly needed something to go their way.

She went to her office door and beckoned to her sergeant. "Hawkes, I've got Uniform looking for Dennison. When he arrives, I want you and I to interview him. I'd like to have a cast-iron case against him but given the lack of evidence that's not going to happen." She handed him the report. "Take a good look, it's full of holes. No sign of anything to start a fire with for starters."

"That vehicle is used by any number of people who work at the gym," Hawkes said. "Any one of them could have driven it to the house and started the fire."

Alice shook her head. "Same old, same old. Our one ace in the hole is that we have him on CCTV. We have the car only one street away from where the Hewsons were living and where the fire was set, but more important, we have a close up of him in the driving seat."

He looked at the still. "The footage is time-stamped within minutes of the fire starting. That means we can place him in the area at the time of the arson attack."

"Exactly," Alice said. "But is it enough to nail him?"

"We'll ask him to explain what he's doing there. Depending on what he tells us, we'll see. Are we prepared to do a deal, ma'am?" Hawkes asked. "If Dennison is guilty, he might offer us Reagan if we go easy on him."

Alice shook her head. "No deals with either of them."

"I don't mean to criticise, ma'am, but isn't that a little short-sighted? Personally, I think that if Dennison offers up Reagan, we should go for it."

Alice thought about this. Hawkes was an excellent officer and he did have a point. Was she being short-sighted? Possibly. She certainly was anxious to get the case wound up. "How about if we see what he comes up with before deciding."

In less than an hour, Alice got word from the front desk that Dennison had been picked up and was on his way in.

"His excuse for us having to go chasing after him was that the gym hadn't been able to get through to him. Him and Reagan were in the depths of Cheshire and reception was bad."

"Rubbish, the man's playing us again," Alice said. "Let me know when he gets here."

She told Hawkes to be ready. "Do we ask about the girls from Ravenswood?" he asked.

"Yes, we have no choice," she said. "He knew them and probably organised the stuff they did for Reagan."

Alice was about to get herself a coffee when Roger Wallis burst into her office.

"Louise Morley has been attacked, ma'am. She was stabbed in Ancoats this afternoon — and in broad daylight too."

"Dennison lives in Ancoats, doesn't he?" Alice said. "Is she badly hurt?"

"Bad enough. She's in theatre now. Though the doctor I spoke to did say that in his opinion she should pull through."

That was something. "I wanted to put her in the safe house but she refused," Alice said. "I should have had her watched, but how d'you do that with someone so involved with a wrong 'un like Dennison?"

"She was under his wing," Wallis said, "so she should have been safe enough. That man has a reputation. I'd have thought no one would dare hurt his girlfriend."

He had a point. "Well one thing we do know, it can't have been him. He's being brought in as we speak, and has been out with Reagan all afternoon."

"We're gathering together all the CCTV we can find," Wallis said. "Birch has had a quick look and has already spotted Louise on her way to an apartment block by the canal. She's being followed by a smallish man dressed in black with his hood pulled up over his head."

Not a description that fitted either Reagan or Dennison, although they could have hired someone to do their dirty work. But who? In her head, Alice ran through a list of likely employees at the gym. Sefton was dead but there was a host of part-timers, all desperate to prove their worth. Reagan had only to ask and they'd jump at the chance.

CHAPTER FORTY-THREE

"Apparently, Dennison is on his own," Hawkes said. "No fancy solicitor with him, which is a surprise. I expected him to have the same one as Reagan."

"Dominic Stubbs is probably a bit too expensive for Dennison," Alice said. "We'll see what he says to the duty solicitor."

The pair entered the room and sat facing Dennison, who was leaning back in his chair as if he didn't have a care in the world.

"You do have the right to have a solicitor present," Alice reminded him.

Dennison simply smiled. "No need, as you'll soon realise."

With a shrug, Alice got on with reciting the formalities for the tape. Then she began. "You've been brought here on a charge of arson."

"Not me. All I've ever set fire to is the family bonfire in November."

"We have that car you drive on CCTV, plus a close-up of you driving only minutes before the fire was set."

Dennison shrugged. "So, I was out in the black estate. As you know, I often use it but that doesn't mean I did whatever you're trying to pin on me."

"Where were you last Friday?" she asked.

"I was working all day at the gym, apart from nipping out briefly on an errand for Max."

"Did this errand involve firebombing a house with a vulnerable family staying in it?"

"No, it did not," he said. "I've told you, you've got the wrong person. I'm not an arsonist."

"Well, that is strange, Mr Dennison, because like I said we can place you a street away from where someone carried out a serious arson attack. Not only that, but the house that was set on fire was sheltering witnesses who were prepared to testify against Reagan, your employer."

Dennison laughed. "You're dreaming if you think any-one in this city will testify against Max. As for me and where I was, you've got the wrong man in the wrong place."

Alice slid a photo across the table. "You, I think. And note the time, just minutes before the house went up in flames. What have you got to say now?"

"What I have to say, Inspector, is that I hope that you have more than this to base your case on."

"I think it's quite enough," Alice said. "Take a good look. It's you all right."

Dennison squinted at it. "So what. It could be someone who looks like me."

Here we go, thought Alice, the get-out tactics. "That's you, and you can't deny it."

"So what if it is. I'm still not guilty of anything."

Alice took a moment, disconcerted. He seemed so sure of himself and given the evidence she'd just shown him, she was beginning to wonder why. "How come you've refused a solicitor?"

"I don't want anyone telling Max that I've been speak-ing to the police," he admitted.

"Why's that then? Are you afraid he'll think you're the bad apple who finally grasses on him? Since you're here, maybe you'd like to tell us something about Reagan's operations."

He smiled. "Not just yet."

177

"What do you mean, 'not just yet'?"

"Oh, nothing." He looked at his watch. "Now, if you've finished with me, I've somewhere to be."

"I'm sorry, Mr Dennison, but you're going nowhere. I intend to detain you for as long as I'm allowed while I double-check the evidence we've got."

"Oh, I wouldn't do that. Definitely the wrong move."

"I don't think so."

Dennison nodded to Hawkes. "Can he be trusted?"

"Of course he can. What a thing to ask. The sergeant is a valued officer," Alice said, somewhat puzzled.

"I want you to speak to someone for me. Do that and you'll understand."

"I don't appreciate riddles, Mr Dennison. Explain what you mean. This someone, is it your solicitor?"

"No, it's Superintendent George Parker from the drugs squad."

CHAPTER FORTY-FOUR

Leaving Dennison with Hawkes, Alice went to her office to make the call. Surprise at what Dennison had just told her didn't cut it, she was positively shocked. Was this man, second only to Reagan in Manchester's drug trade, really working for the police?

It turned out that he was. Parker was furious that his operative had been brought into the station. "Get the bugger back on the streets now," he ordered. "And for God's sake don't blow his cover — you'll get him killed."

"We think he committed arson, sir," Alice said.

"Ridiculous," Parker snapped. "Dennison is a bit of a maverick but he knows not to overstep the mark. Ask him about the incident — I'm sure he'll have an explanation — and then release him. Quietly."

Suitably contrite, Alice went back to the interview room. "It seems you're right, you are working for Parker. How is that working out?"

"So far, just fine," he said. "Someone has to do it. As long as he doesn't find out, I'm safe enough."

"Why, though? Why you of all people? You're the last person I would have suspected."

"Exactly," he said. "That's what keeps me safe. I've no intention of telling you why I was chosen, not yet, but you'd understand if you knew."

"Okay," said Alice. "Can you at least tell me what did happen when that house was burned down?"

"I was in the black estate following the real culprit. He was driving an old van that also belongs to the gym. I didn't know what he was up to until it was too late. There was nothing I could do to stop him."

"Who was it?" Alice asked.

"I can give you his name though he's no good to you now — he's dead. Reagan doesn't like loose ends."

"Are you talking about Sefton?" she asked.

"No. Sefton had been seen before the house was burned. The fire was set by another one of Reagan's people, a lad called Alec Holden. He was an addict. Holden would do anything for a fix, even kill."

"Dead or not, we'll still have to investigate."

"Just don't mention my name. You'll find plenty of evidence in his locker — and that one is kept locked," Dennison said.

"Do you know why Sefton had to die?" Alice asked.

"He had a loose mouth, or so Reagan said. And he had his fingers in the till. Reagan won't have that."

"We have something recovered from Sefton's flat that might prove useful to your investigation. It's a notebook full of figures that we can't make head nor tail of. Hawkes, would you make sure he gets it before he leaves." She turned back to Dennison. "Our forensic team are still searching Sefton's flat. If they get anything else we'll pass it on."

Now for the big one. "D'you know about Louise?"

He shook his head.

"Earlier today she was attacked near your apartment. She's in the infirmary having surgery, but I'm told she's not too badly hurt." She noticed how upset Dennison looked.

"You'll be released soon so you'll be able to get down there. We'll follow on shortly. She may have seen her attacker."

Dennison shook his head. "Why would anyone want to attack Louise? Is this to do with me, d'you reckon?"

"We don't think so. You see, Louise was one of a group of five girls, four of whom have been murdered. That is our main focus, the Reagan case has simply got us sidetracked."

"Did these girls work for Reagan?" Dennison asked.

"Yes, they were runners. But we don't believe that's the reason why they were killed. There's something else going on there but we're struggling to find out what. Maybe it's down to another dealer, someone they worked for before Reagan. I was hoping Louise would be able to help us."

Dennison made for the door. "I'll have a word with her if she's up to it. As for Reagan, if Parker has anything to do with it his reign should be over soon. There's a large consignment coming in and when it does, Parker will strike. I just need to tell him when."

Important work, Alice realised. On her way to her office, she passed Wallis in the incident room. He gave her a funny look.

"I've just seen Dennison leaving, ma'am. Surely, the evidence we had was enough to nail him."

"Leave it, Constable. Now is not the time. You and Birch take a couple of uniformed officers and go to Reagan's gym. Search the locker of one Alec Holden and confiscate what you find. Don't be fobbed off when you're told that it's used by everyone, because it isn't. This particular locker was used by Holden alone. And don't bother looking for Holden either, he's dead."

Alice went into her office and shut the door. She needed time to think, to go over what she'd just learned. After a few minutes, she called to Hawkes.

"It goes without saying that what Dennison told us is not to be repeated," she said. "I want you to examine the CCTV footage from around Dennison's apartment. Someone was seen following Louise and since it wasn't Dennison, see if you can spot anything that might help us identify who it might be."

"Do you have anyone in mind, ma'am?"

Alice shook her head. "We've ruled out most of the likely suspects. Study that footage and see what you think."

CHAPTER FORTY-FIVE

Now what? He'd failed and all because he'd been forced to act too fast, taking chances. With the others he'd had time, wearing them down, readying himself to strike. This one had been different. Could she have recognised him? Unlikely, but it was still a possibility. Now he had no option but to try again, and this time he would make sure the girl was dead before he left her.

He rifled through his wardrobe looking for something suitable to wear for the hospital. Somewhere in here there was a set of medical scrubs he'd acquired on a previous visit with an eye to their future use. They were just what he needed to give him access to Louise Morley.

This time he wouldn't use a knife. He needed a method more in keeping with her current surroundings. He took a syringe from a drawer and checked it. Perfect. An overdose of morphine should do to finish her off neatly. Not only would it kill the girl but it would also send the police off on the wrong track. He knew all about their obsession with Max Reagan. This would make an interesting little addition to their evidence against him. They'd look at the method and go after the drug dealer.

* * *

"See the shadow, ma'am?" Hawkes pointed to something in the corner of the image. "I reckon the bloke following Louise is being followed himself."

Alice peered at the screen. Hawkes could be right. "Can we get this blown up?"

"Already on it, ma'am, but look at the second man. Look at the shape of his body and his the way he moves. He's young. Athletic."

"Who are you thinking of?" Alice asked.

"My instincts tell me Freddie Whitton, although we could do with speaking to Louise first. She might recall some detail that will help us."

"Then we'll go and speak to her right away," Alice said.

Since the hospital was practically on the doorstep they went there on foot.

"Do we know if she's out of theatre and conscious?" Alice asked as they strode along.

"She is, ma'am. Birch rang the ward earlier. The wound wasn't too deep and the operation went well. She should make a full recovery."

This was good news. Alice desperately wanted to protect Louise and keep her from suffering the same fate as the others. "We have to give her protection. We have to ensure that whoever stabbed her doesn't get to her a second time."

"There's the safe house, ma'am."

"I'll see what she says. Meanwhile we have posted a guard outside her room. Dennison won't be able to stay with her all the time."

Passing the guard on their way into the room, she said, "Make sure she's not left for a moment. I'll get someone to take over in a couple of hours' time so you can get yourself something to eat."

Dennison was already there, sitting by the bed and holding her hand. "Sorry to intrude, Louise," Alice said gently. "I know you probably don't feel like talking right now, but for your own safety it's important that we catch whoever attacked you."

"I don't mind," Louise said. "As a matter of fact, talking about it helps. I need to get the whole scary episode off my chest so I don't keep thinking about it."

"Is there anything at all you can tell us about him?"

"He came out of nowhere and struck me from behind," she said. "One thing I do remember is that he smelled strange."

"Aftershave, something like that?" Alice asked.

Louise shook her head. "No, it wasn't a pleasant smell. It was like his clothes were musty, though underneath it there was a scent I recognised because Freddie wears it. I also recall hearing a voice telling me not to worry, to go to sleep. I thought I knew the voice too, but I can't remember whose it is now."

What she'd just told them got Alice thinking. "D'you think it was Freddie who attacked you? Maybe it was him who spoke to you too if you thought you knew the voice."

Louise looked away. "I'm not sure. I do associate that fragrance with him and also the voice telling me not to worry. But I couldn't swear to it. I know Freddie and his reputation, so I might have imagined it."

"Anything else? Did you hear him following you?"

"Not really, but it was a sunny afternoon and I could see shadows. Two of them, sort of blending together."

Alice gave Hawkes a look. The shadows on the CCTV that he'd pointed out to her. "But you didn't turn round and look?"

Louise shook her head.

"He attacked you near to the canal. Our forensics people are there, so if there's anything to find, they will."

"The canal . . ." Louise said thoughtfully. "Yes, I remember now. I did see something, a reflection." She looked up at the detectives and Dennison and started to shake.

"It's all right, Louise, we're with you. Just tell us."

Now she was weeping. "I was supposed to die, wasn't I? I know that now. I've remembered, you see. I can see him, I know what he looked like."

"Who, Louise? Who did you see?" Alice asked.

"A ghost. I saw a ghost."

CHAPTER FORTY-SIX

"She has to be joking, surely," Hawkes said to Alice on their way back from the hospital.

"She's confused, probably mildly concussed," Alice said. "But we'll bring Freddie Whitton in. It'll do no harm to find out where he was when Louise was attacked."

"What about his mate, Laser? Shouldn't we have a go at him too?"

"We'll see what Freddie has to say for himself first."

Hawkes's mobile rang. "It's Wallis, ma'am. They found a pile of stuff in Holden's locker including clothing. Wallis is having it tested for accelerant."

"Well done. Shame he's dead. With the prospect of prison hanging over him he might have given us Reagan," Alice said. "We'll have to make enquiries about what happened to the lad. It'll mean more questions for Reagan and he won't like that. But first we'll speak to Freddie."

"D'you want him bringing in? Hawkes asked.

"No, let's keep it casual, we might get more out of him that way. We'll visit him at his flat."

* * *

The area around Freddie's flat was busy with groups of kids milling around. As the detectives got out of the car, one of the kids pointed to them and whispered to his mate.

"Make sure the car's locked up tight," Alice told Hawkes. "That lot are villains in the making."

Hawkes walked across to them. Alice had no idea what he'd said but it did the trick. The group scarpered as fast as their legs could carry them.

Alice smiled at him. "I bet Uniform were upset when they lost you."

"Probably. But I was happy to go," he said.

He banged on the door and Freddie appeared almost immediately. "Is this about Louise?"

"Is that a good guess, Freddie, or do you have a reason for asking?" Alice said.

"I was there," he said, standing aside for them to go in. "It was me who called the ambulance, and I stayed with her until I saw them coming up the road."

"Want to tell us about it?" Alice asked. "You should have come and given us a statement. You witnessed a serious crime. Louise is lucky not to have been killed."

"I was scared too," he said. "I was afraid you'd think it was me who did that to her."

Alice fixed him with a stare. "And was it? Did you attack Louise?"

"No, not me. I wouldn't do a thing like that," he said.

"Then why were you following her?"

"I didn't want her to get hurt."

"And you thought she might," Alice said. "You knew very well that someone had Louise in his sights. I want to know who that is, Freddie. Refuse to tell me and I'll lock you up."

Freddie shook his head. "I don't know, really, not for sure. I didn't see his face either. He had it covered up."

"I'm not sure I believe you," Alice said. "Part of what you've told us is true, we have it on CCTV. Unfortunately that only shows shadows. However, I think you know more about what happened than you're telling me."

Alice paused, giving him a moment to think about what she'd said. "Come on, Freddie. I want answers. Tell me what you know."

"Look, I can't tell you what I don't know. But one thing is certain, I didn't harm Louise. Why would I? All I wanted to do was make sure she was safe, that's why I was following her. That's it, there's nothing else I can tell you."

"How did you know she was in danger?" Alice asked.

"It was something Dennison said. Louise had told him she was the last survivor of a group of girls. There were five of them to begin with and the others are all dead, murdered and buried in Ravenswood."

Alice watched him. Okay, he'd admitted to being present when Louise was stabbed but there was something not quite right about what he was telling them.

"Ellie Fleming got threatening letters. Did you read them?" she asked.

"Spooky things in old-fashioned writing," he said.

"Have you any idea what those girls knew?" she asked him. "Because whatever it was got them murdered. Someone is trying hard to hide something and has killed to keep it a secret."

"Look, I don't know anything about that. I saw what was happening and I rushed over to help Louise, that's all."

"Those letters Ellie was sent, they were written with materials acquired from your uncle Ralph's office."

"I know that but we've been told that Laser's girlfriend stole the equipment. She works at Kendrick's and so had access to your uncle's office."

"There you are then, speak to Laser," he said.

"We already have. We know he got the stuff for someone but he wouldn't say who." Alice gave the young man a moment. "Laser got the writing materials for you, didn't he? What I don't understand is why. Why write all those letters to Ellie Fleming? You even sent one to us."

"I wrote one letter, the last one she got. I wanted Ellie to wake up, realise the danger she was in." He looked Alice in the eye. "She stayed with us for a while. I loved her and wanted to keep her safe. I failed and I blame myself for that."

Alice saw the tears in his eyes, the admission had come from the heart. "You're telling me you're not responsible for the other letters, or the one sent to the station?"

"That wasn't down to me, I promise."

"Why d'you work for Max Reagan? Surely you must know that the gym is a cover for his drug dealing."

Freddie sighed. "I know what he is. Reagan is the new drug baron in this city. I used to work for the last one too. I'm not proud of it but I needed the money."

That got Alice's interest. "Did you now. Tell me then, who was Reagan's predecessor?"

"I never knew his real name, everyone just called him Butcher."

"Come on, you can do better than that. Weren't you curious at all?"

Freddie shook his head. "I truly have no idea. All his transactions were carried out by runners or over the phone."

"Do you still have any of the phone numbers?" Alice asked.

"We used burner phones and destroyed them."

Alice had heard enough. They were getting nowhere. "We'll talk about your old boss again. For now, I'm more interested in the letters."

"Like I said, I wrote one, and that's all."

Was he lying? Alice couldn't tell. Her instinct was to believe him. Freddie had been straight with them so far. Was he being straight now, or was he simply a clever liar?

CHAPTER FORTY-SEVEN

"If you want my opinion, we should have arrested him, ma'am," Hawkes said when they'd left the flat.

"Wrong move. We'll keep an eye on him. I'm still in two minds about whether he's hurt anyone," Alice said. "I believe Freddie Whitton is telling us some of the truth but it's what he's not saying that interests me more. Whatever it is, my gut tells me it's vital to the case."

Alice saw from the dubious look he gave her that Hawkes had little faith in her gut.

"Where to now? Want to have another word with Laser?" he asked.

"Back to the station. Following on from what we've just been told, I've got some questions for Forensics. Someone should be able to tell us if the writer of that last letter is different from the person who wrote the rest."

"Okay, if we accept that Freddie only wrote the last letter, who wrote the rest?"

Alice gave him a grim smile. "The person we've been looking for, Sergeant. Our killer. I can't see it being anyone else."

While Hawkes drove them back, Alice sat in silence, weighing up what Freddie had told them. A former kingpin known as Butcher. Not very original. She wondered why he'd been so keen to hide his identity. Was he well known? Something to ponder over.

Back in her office, she gave Tony Birch the task of getting some background on this man. Then she rang Jack Nevin.

"The letters," she began, "I have reason to believe that the last one I gave you was written by someone else. I have Freddie Whitton in mind."

"If that's so, have you considered how Freddie knew the exact paper, pen and ink that had been used to produce the others?" he said.

Alice had to admit that she hadn't. "What are you getting at?"

"It's all very well having an example of the previous letters, but unless you know where to find the same stationery, you won't get very far."

"Both his uncles use stuff like that, so he could have known," Alice said.

"Close to his uncles, is he?"

"He says not. I've just spoken to Freddie and he denies having anything to do with them. Reckons he's never been to that office."

"All the letters, including the last one, are written on the same sort of paper. I think Freddie has been telling you lies."

"Don't say that, Jack. I was hoping that whoever wrote all but one of those letters is our killer, and he's not Freddie Whitton."

"I sent them away to be analysed and have now received the report back. Everything is a match — paper, ink, the lot. Also, all the letters, including the last one, were written in the same hand."

This meant that Freddie was their phantom letter-writer. But what she couldn't figure out was why. "Thanks, Jack. That clears things up."

It also angered Alice. Did Freddie know the identity of their killer and for reasons of his own was protecting him? Why would he do that?

She marched into the incident room. "Have you got anything on this Butcher yet?" she asked Tony Birch.

"There's not much. He was a small-time dealer who ran a county lines operation for a while. Once Reagan came on the scene, he simply disappeared. We've heard nothing since. It's as if he evaporated into thin air."

They needed to find this man Butcher. She had plenty of questions to ask him. But she had other things on her mind right now. "Go and arrest Freddie Whitton. No argument, just bring him in."

"Your gut giving you trouble, ma'am?" Hawkes quipped.

Alice shot him a disapproving look. "This is no time to joke, Sergeant. I don't think Freddie killed anyone but I am convinced he knows who did."

* * *

There was a police guard on the door. Of course, there was, she was an important witness. *Keep your nerve*, he told himself. *This is too important to get wrong*.

With a nod to the guard, he entered the room. Seeing the scrubs, the man hadn't given him a second look. He stood over the sleeping Louise Morley.

But first, in case he was being watched, he checked the dials on the equipment. They meant nothing to him. Was she doing well? He reckoned so. The chart on the wall above her bed gave all her observations as normal. She could be discharged at any time.

He touched the syringe in his pocket, filled with a deadly dose of morphine. Everything was set. All he had to do was push it into her arm and she'd trouble him no more.

"Everything okay?"

He spun round to see a nurse standing in the doorway. "Don't wake her," she whispered. "She had trouble getting off."

He had no choice. He wasn't about to take on a nurse. He nodded and backed away.

"Are you new?" the nurse asked, taking the chart from the wall. "You must be, I've not seen you before. I can't keep up anymore. These days the staff changes by the minute."

He nodded again.

"Is there anything else you need?" she asked. "Only I'm about to sort her stuff for going home."

Thwarted at every turn. He wanted to scream. "I'll leave you to it then," he said and turned to go.

The guard stopped him as he passed through the door.

"Excuse me, sir. I need to take your name and which department in the hospital you're based in."

"Look, I'm in a hurry. My bleeper has just gone off and I'm needed in theatre. I'll come back later and give you my details."

The policeman hesitated for a moment. "Okay, but don't forget."

CHAPTER FORTY-EIGHT

"I'm getting a little tired of this."

"You're not the only one, Freddie. But you tell us the truth and we'll stop bothering you," Alice said. "You can start by telling me why you lied about the letters."

"I didn't. I wrote the last one and I've no idea who wrote the others."

"You're lying again. I've had them analysed and the expert tells me all the letters were written by the same person. That means you, Freddie. And don't try to wriggle out of it. You gave a statement about your whereabouts on the day Maggie disappeared. The handwriting expert checked it against the letters."

Freddie took this in, shrugged, looked around the incident room and took a swig of water from the glass in front of him. "You're wrong. I'm innocent. I don't lie."

"Oh, but you do, Freddie. You lie so well you took me in. I think that over time you actually come to believe those lies yourself." Alice wanted to slap the stupid grin off his face. The young man was a practised liar, he damn well knew what he'd done. "You play a good game, Freddie, but your luck is running out."

There was little reaction. He took another swig of water. "Can I have a solicitor now? I don't think I should say anything else without taking advice. Next thing you'll be pinning those killings on me."

There was an odd look in eyes, a look that made Alice wonder exactly what his part in all this was. "Any solicitor in particular?"

"Dominic Stubbs," he said.

"He's expensive," Hawkes warned. "Sorry to be personal but you're not working at the moment."

"Reagan will pay."

He seemed very sure of this. "Is that so you don't drop him in it?" Alice asked dryly. "Believe me, Freddie, Reagan is going to get his, regardless of what you tell us."

Alice stood up, gathered her paperwork together and left the room followed by Hawkes.

"Irritating as it is, we have no choice but to wait until Stubbs gets here," she said on their way back to the incident room. "I'm in no mood for any more lies. I want the truth or I'll detain Freddie on suspicion of murder and attacking Louise."

"He denies it all, ma'am."

"Yes, and he's probably telling the truth about that. Nevertheless, he knows something, and the more he lies the more important I think that something is. He needs pushing or we'll never get the truth out of him."

* * *

Back in the incident room, Wallis was sitting at his desk looking particularly pleased with himself. As soon as Alice entered the room he called her over. "The police guard looking out for Louise can't be sure but he thinks an unauthorised person has been in her room."

Alice threw the file she was carrying onto the nearest desk. She was annoyed. Guarding a door was simple enough. "What's wrong with these people? Have they no brains! No one should be allowed in that room without showing him proper identification first. Has she been harmed?"

"Apparently not, he was interrupted by a nurse. Whoever he was, he was wearing hospital scrubs so the guard assumed he was a doctor. To be fair, ma'am, it's an easy mistake to make. It was only when the man wouldn't give his details on leaving the room that the guard got suspicious."

"Can he give a description of this man?"

"Better than that, ma'am. The guard was wearing his bodycam and got a recording of him. He's sent me a copy. It's all set up ready."

This was the break they needed. Alice felt the load on her shoulders immediately lighten. If this was their killer trying to have another go at Louise, then they had him. "Right then, let's have a look."

The team crowded round Wallis's computer screen and he started the film. It was short and both parties hardly spoke. But there was no mistaking who they were looking at.

When it was over the atmosphere among the team was electric. Hawkes gave a little whistle. "That explains what Louise said about her attacker."

"How do you mean?" Alice said.

"She said he was a ghost." He pointed at the figure on the screen. "Look at him. He's a dead ringer for a spook. I thought that the first time I set eyes on him."

CHAPTER FORTY-NINE

Alice and Hawkes went back along the corridor to speak to Freddie again. Now Alice knew for sure that he hadn't been straight with them — what she'd just seen on that snippet of film was proof of that.

She marched into the interview room, slammed the door shut and faced him, hands on hips. "You should have told me. He's had another go at Louise. If he'd succeeded, you'd be in even more trouble than you already are, and what's more, he's still out there."

Freddie stared at her, wide-eyed. "You have to stop him. He'll kill her if he gets to her again."

Alice sat down. "Why protect him? I don't understand."

"Because I'm too involved," he said. "I have been since the start so he'll never let me go. You don't know him like I do. He's a madman but he means what he says. When my Uncle Felix says he'll kill you, he will."

Alice shook her head. Felix Kendrick, the brother who was always ill, who had seemed so charming when they met.

"He killed those girls in cold blood, without a second thought," Freddie went on. "He told me all about it. How they screamed and what he did to them."

"You should have come to us," Alice said.

197

"I tried to tell Reagan. I thought he might take him out but he just laughed at me." Freddie rolled up his sleeve and showed Alice a long, wide scar on his arm. "That was Felix. I needed a dozen stitches and couldn't use the arm for weeks."

Alice had no sympathy. "What was this thing the girls knew that caused him to murder them?"

"Felix killed my mother," Freddie said quietly. "Ellie, Louise and the others saw him burying her and tackled him about it. They worked for him as drug runners, so he started by promising them more money to keep them quiet. Then he set about systematically destroying them."

"Hawkes," Alice said to her sergeant. "I want Felix Kendrick bringing in. And double the watch on Louise Morley."

She turned back to Freddie. "You still haven't said why you were protecting him."

"I've just told you."

"I don't believe you. You weren't that afraid. There's something else, has to be."

"Has my solicitor arrived yet?" he said.

"Even Stubbs can't get you out of this one," Alice said. "Why don't you tell me what was really going on, Freddie? It can only go in your favour in the end."

He buried his face in his hands. "It was the dealing. I was up to my neck in it. It was me organised the county lines and recruited the runners. I also arranged the supply of drugs from the big dealers."

"I thought Reagan was the main dealer in this city," Alice said.

"He is, but there's plenty of room for others, particularly out in the sticks like where Felix lives. He's got those villages completely sewn up. I've helped him over the last few years, and he holds that over me." He raised his head and looked beseechingly at Alice. "I talk to you and he'll make sure I suffer for it. If he doesn't kill me before then, he'll make sure someone gets to me in prison. Felix knows people that owe him and he won't shy away from calling in a favour or two."

There was a knock on the door and Birch stuck his head in. "The Kendrick house is empty, ma'am, and he's not at the factory."

Alice looked at Freddie. "Where's he likely to go? Does he have a bolt-hole? Come on, Freddie. Felix needs bringing in before he kills again."

Freddie shook his head. "I don't know of anywhere. He's usually at home."

"Try harder. We have to find him."

There was another knock. This time it was Roger Wallis. "There's something going on in Ravenswood, ma'am. The residents in the water board cottages have heard gunshots."

Ravenswood. "Is that where he put your mother?" Alice asked Freddie.

He nodded.

"Lock him up until I return," she told Wallis. "Stubbs turns up, tell him he'll have to wait."

Alice ran to the incident room and grabbed her jacket and phone. "You and me, Hawkes."

"If there's shooting going on, shouldn't we organise armed backup?" he said.

He was right but Alice was loath to wait. She knew that if Felix took on the police marksmen, he'd lose, and she wanted to bring him in.

"Get it organised," she told Birch.

CHAPTER FIFTY

It was getting dark and had been raining all day. Ravenswood was a quagmire. The woods were extensive and they'd no idea where to start searching. Instinctively, the pair made for the clearing where the girls had been buried.

Their instincts were correct. Crouched over a patch of bare ground, Felix Kendrick appeared to be talking to himself.

"It's over, Felix. Time to come with us," Hawkes shouted.

Kendrick turned to face them. Underneath his raincoat they could see he was still wearing the hospital scrubs. Alice moved closer. "We know what you've done and we know about Louise. There's nowhere to go. It's over, Felix."

He stood up. "I never did like you."

The venom in his voice chilled Alice to the bone.

"When you first took the case on, I knew you'd be trouble, so I gathered all the information I could find on you. You've been stalking me like a curse, never allowing me a minute's rest."

"Is this where you buried Fiona?" Hawkes said.

With his eyes on Alice, he said. "Ah, sweet Fiona, my beautiful sister. She too had a poisoned mouth." The smile he directed at Alice was evil. "She knew, you see. She knew what me and Freddie had done. In time, she would probably have forgiven Freddie — but me? Never."

Felix struggled to his feet, almost slipping on the wet ground. Then they saw the shotgun. He raised it, slowly.

"Don't be stupid," Hawkes said. "You'll only make things worse for yourself."

Felix shook his head. "I doubt that. Things are so bad already they can't get any worse. My case gets to court and the entire country will hate me. I murdered four teenage girls in cold blood — worse, I imprisoned and tortured them first. I am the devil incarnate. Two more will not make a jot of difference."

Alice's stomach was turning somersaults. What could they do? She didn't doubt for one second that he'd use the gun.

"You're making a mistake," Hawkes tried again, stepping in front of her.

"Ooh, look at you. Quite the gentleman, aren't you?" Felix said. "No matter. I'll shoot you down first and then I'll take great pleasure in finishing her."

"No!" Hawkes shouted. He took a step forward. A shot rang out and Hawkes hit the ground.

She knelt beside him, trying to find where he'd been hit. This was her fault. They'd rushed off here without waiting for backup and this was the result.

Felix inched closer. He licked his lips, a mad grin on his face. Alice closed her eyes. She had a wild notion of making a grab for his legs but he was just out of reach.

A second shot pierced the quiet of the wood. Alice was certain that she too must have been shot but she felt no pain. Opening her eyes, she saw that Hawkes was now sitting up. He was clutching his upper arm. She leaned over to him.

"I'm okay," he insisted. "What happened?"

"I have no idea." Then she saw him, standing on the path a few metres behind Felix, who was now lying face down in the mud. "Ralph! Is he dead?"

Ralph Kendrick bent down and felt for a pulse. "Yes. It's over. He won't harm anyone else."

"I didn't know you had a gun," Alice said.

"It's perfectly legal, the paperwork is in order. I use it for killing rats."

* * *

Jason Hawkes was treated in hospital for a flesh wound and was out of action for the time being. Not that that stopped him from going into the station to find out how Alice was.

"Ralph Kendrick saved our bacon," she said. "If he hadn't been there, well, I dread to think."

"What about Freddie?" Hawkes asked.

"Under arrest. When Stubbs saw what we'd got on him he turned tail and left. Freddie Whitton is on his own, I'm afraid. No help from Reagan and certainly none from his uncle."

"Has he said where Felix kept the girls?" Hawkes asked.

Alice shook her head. "He says he doesn't know but he could be lying. Ralph assures me it can't have been the family home. It's large but it's well alarmed and has numerous cameras, even in the cellars. However, we've got a team looking again at the factory. There are parts of that building that haven't been used in years."

Alice told the team to go home. "It's been a long, hard day. We'll have a briefing in the morning when Superintendent Monk is around. He'll want to know every detail about what happened."

"You all right to drive?" Hawkes asked her.

"A strong cuppa and I'll be fine," she assured him. "And I don't want to see you until that arm is healed."

He winked at her. "We'll see."

CHAPTER FIFTY-ONE

Tuesday

Tired as she was, Alice hardly slept. Every time she closed her eyes she saw Felix Kendrick brandishing that shotgun.

"Are you ill?" Dilys asked, looking at the circles under her eyes.

"No, just overworked and overwrought. It'll pass, it usually does."

"I'll make us something nice for tea," Dilys said. "We'll open a bottle of wine, cheer you up."

Alice smiled at her. "You're a real tonic, you are. I don't know what I'd do without you."

Alice left for work at about seven thirty. On the way in, she rang Hawkes to ask how he was.

"I kept having nightmares," he admitted. "That bloody maniac, staring at me."

"Same here," Alice said. "But we don't need to worry about him anymore, he's gone, and the case is solved."

"Except for Freddie."

"He'll be charged, don't worry. I'm speaking to Monk this morning, then I'll brief the team," she said.

"Mind if I come?"

"You're on sick leave, Hawkes. You should be resting."

"It'll do my head in being at home all day with nothing to do."

"Okay, but you sit at your desk, and no brain work."

* * *

Alice took the lift up to Leo Monk's office. She expected him to be pleased that the case was finally over, but how would he react to the fact that their main culprit was dead?

"You went in there without armed backup," he said straight off. "You'd been told he had a gun, so why didn't you wait?"

"We were told that shots had been heard in the woods. We weren't to know it was Felix Kendrick doing the shooting," she said.

"And the man who shot him?"

"His brother, Ralph."

He wasn't being fair. She had to make him see how it had been. "Hawkes and I were staring down the barrel of a shotgun," she said. "Felix told us straight out that he intended to shoot us, and he did. He winged Hawkes and then aimed the gun at me. I heard another shot and for a moment I believed he'd got me."

Alice could feel the tears pricking her eyes. The last thing she wanted was to break down in front of Monk. She swallowed hard. "If it wasn't for Ralph, Hawkes and I would have been dead. Ralph saved us both."

"Well, you were both lucky but the fact remains that you should not have been in that situation. However, Armed Response was on your tail."

Oh, were they? Alice didn't recall seeing them. Shock, she presumed.

"The search of the factory has proved interesting," Leo Monk said. "There are several cellars where the girls could have been held. Forensics are doing their job as we speak."

"And Ralph or the workforce didn't know?"

"They were well hidden. There were a stack of boxes in front of what we finally discovered was a small door. These aren't ordinary cellars, either, they are deep underground. Ralph told me they were intended as bomb shelters during the war."

Alice shuddered at the thought of being imprisoned somewhere like that. "Am I needed up there, sir?" she asked, crossing her fingers. She really didn't want to go.

"It won't be pleasant. I suggest you read the forensic report instead."

"I'll be sure to scrutinise it for any evidence that Freddie Whitton was there," she said, relieved to be let off the hook. "That young man has lied through his eye teeth throughout. It'll be a pleasure to throw the book at him."

* * *

Alice returned to the incident room to be met with cheers and whoops.

"Max Reagan has been arrested," a jubilant Roger Wallis told her. "Charged with drug dealing and murder."

This was good news indeed, but what had happened to make Parker decide to act? "How come?" she asked. "When?"

"Forensics found more evidence under Sefton's floor-boards, notably a mobile with snippets of conversations and a video of Max battering a young lad, who we have identified as a missing teenager who used to go to Reagan's gym. When he'd finished kicking the lad, he took a pistol and shot him in the head, and then put him in a bin at the back of the gym. Forensics have been all over it and found traces of the lad's blood. Reagan's prints were all over it. The same blood was also found on a pair of Reagan's trainers."

"He'll deny it," Alice said. "He and Stubbs are bound to tell Parker that the lad's death was down to someone else."

"They can deny it all they like but I don't think he's going to wriggle out of this one," Wallis said.

Alice could only hope that the CPS took the case forward. It was about time Reagan got his.

"The body of Fiona Whitton has been found, ma'am," Birch told her. "She was buried in the place Hawkes suggested they look."

Alice was relieved. At last, Fiona's husband could move on.

"Case over then," she declared. "Now I'd better get the reports written. I'll be in my office and I want no interruptions unless someone brings me coffee. You've all done well. We'll have a celebratory drink in the Beaufort Arms later."

EPILOGUE

Keen to get home to Dilys, Alice didn't stay long in the Beaufort. The woman had spent enough time on her own and her sister's funeral was looming.

The minute Alice was through the front door, Dilys pushed a wadge of brown envelopes into her hand. "These came for you. They're from that estate agents in town. What're you playing at?"

What to tell her? Alice had hoped to keep this to herself for a while but the cat was now out of the bag. "I'm thinking of selling this house and buying something smaller."

That didn't go down well. Dilys immediately burst into tears.

"I've been coming to this house ever since you were born," she wailed. "You can't possibly leave it now."

"It's fast becoming unmanageable, Dilys. There are rooms upstairs I never use. There's a sitting room down here I never venture into. I'm not looking to go too far away. I thought Burnage, which'll be handy for work, and either the city or Stockport."

"But what about me? No way is Burnage going to be handy for me."

"I know you're not happy where you are, Dilys. You don't want to go home, so why not move in with me permanently?"

Dilys smiled at Alice through her tears. "D'you really mean that? You won't get fed up with me after a while?"

"No way. I'd love to have you around all the time."

Alice watched her face clear. Dilys liked the idea. "I thought we'd go and look at a couple of properties this weekend."

"We?" Dilys said.

"Of course. You'll have a say in it too."

Alice was about to pour the wine when they were interrupted by the front door bell. Dilys went to answer it and returned with Leo Monk in tow. Then she left them to it.

"Is everything all right, sir?"

He cleared his throat. "You did well with the Dream Catcher case."

Though Alice was thankful for the praise, the look on Monk's face told her this wasn't all. He wasn't making a social call. "It was a close thing," she said. "We had a lot of luck."

"Well, Dream Catcher was something of a cold case. I wonder if you can handle a more recent one."

Alice felt her stomach tighten. "Er, what did you have in mind?"

"D'you recall the Penrose murders?" Monk asked.

Alice did indeed. It was hard to forget that dreadful case. A middle-aged married couple had been burned to death in their bed.

"Then you'll recall that no one was ever apprehended," Monk said.

"I seem to remember there were several suspects though," she said.

"But no real evidence," Monk said.

"You want me to start from scratch?"

"The Penrose killings happened five years ago. The week before last another couple was killed in exactly the same way."

Alice felt a shiver down her spine. Everyone had hoped the Penrose murders were a one-off. Apparently not.

"Can you be sure it's the same killer? Isn't one house fire much like another?"

"I take your point, Alice, but there were certain aspects of the Penrose case that only we and the killer are aware of. They were never made public."

Alice took the file he handed her. This was it, their next case. "I'll have a read and brief the team tomorrow."

"If anyone can get this killer it's you, Alice. I have every confidence in your ability."

Now this really was praise.

THE END

THE JOFFE BOOKS STORY

We began in 2014 when Jasper agreed to publish his mum's much-rejected romance novel and it became a bestseller.

Since then we've grown into the largest independent publisher in the UK. We're extremely proud to publish some of the very best writers in the world, including Joy Ellis, Faith Martin, Caro Ramsay, Helen Forrester, Simon Brett and Robert Goddard. Everyone at Joffe Books loves reading and we never forget that it all begins with the magic of an author telling a story.

We are proud to publish talented first-time authors, as well as established writers whose books we love introducing to a new generation of readers.

We have been shortlisted for Independent Publisher of the Year at the British Book Awards three times, in 2020, 2021 and 2022, and for the Diversity and Inclusivity Award at the Independent Publishing Awards in 2022.

We built this company with your help, and we love to hear from you, so please email us about absolutely anything bookish at: feedback@joffebooks.com.

If you want to receive free books every Friday and hear about all our new releases, join our mailing list: www.joffebooks.com/contact

And when you tell your friends about us, just remember: it's pronounced Joffe as in coffee or toffee!

Milton Keynes UK
Ingram Content Group UK Ltd.
UKHW010633101123
432322UK00006B/300